The Goblin Pitcher

Paul Lonardo Copyright 2021
www.thegoblinpitcher.com

PL
Publishing

Illustrations by Avery Palmer

Cover design by The Book Cover Whisperer

For my son, I grow prouder of you every day.

On Tiv-ra Hill near Cushendall,
I heard a commotion behind a wall,
I stopped and looked over, and boys-o-boys!
Now what do you think was making the noise?

'Twas a Hurley match- and may I choke-
It was two wee teams of the Fairy folk
That was ripplin' and tearin' and weltin' away
In the light of the moon as bright as day.

~ H.Browne

PREGAME

From the moment Jake Lupo arrived in Pine Barrows with his parents, he knew there was something different about the remote, mountain forest community. He was eleven going on twelve, but he had lived in many different parts of the country as his father worked his way up through the minor league ranks of professional baseball. Many of the places they resided in over the years were small towns, but none of them had been this far off the beaten path, and none had induced such strange feelings in Jake or been host to so many unusual sights and sounds.

In the city, there was a continuous mechanical drone from cars, ambulances, police sirens, construction machinery, and millions of collective voices. The country, however, had a resonance all its own. In harmony with the natural world; the trees, the wind, birds, insects, plants and animals, there lies an undertone of hidden activity, and reverberations from an abundance of life that exist in an array of forms, some dwelling in a magical realm that few are able to observe. Jake could always see what he thought to be goblins, though he didn't always believe what his eyes revealed to him.

When he was in a forest or a park, he would sometimes see them in the pattern of the wood on the trees. He would glimpse their faces etched in craggy rocks or stumps, a bulbous nose in the knot of a tree trunk, pointy ears formed from the leaves of a flowering shrub, hairy torsos of sleepy goblins lying on the ground among the moss and lichen. Occasionally, an entire goblin would take shape, and a few times he had seen them moving about. Most vivid in his mind was when he was six-years old, running around a playground in Central Park. The sun had been setting, and it was just beginning to get dark when he briefly wandered away from his parents. Behind a large rock, he saw something very odd. About twenty little men, no bigger than him, came marching toward him in single file. They were dressed in leather knee pants held up by suspenders. They wore no shirts. They were hairless, and their skin was pale. They were humming a strange tune as they passed by, paying no attention to him.

One by one, they departed around the other end of the rock. A moment later his father appeared from the exact same spot calling his name, so Jake knew that his father had not seen the strange little men. He never told his father, or anyone else, what he had seen that day. He chalked it up to an overactive imagination, which was what his mother had always told him whenever he tried to tell her about something unusual that he had seen or heard.

Jake didn't know what to expect in Pine Barrows, but the inhabitants of Pine Barrows were sure expecting him.

Top of the 1st

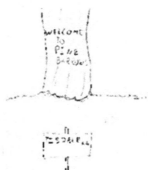

It was a long drive from the city, but only an hour into the trip Jake began to lose the signal on his phone and tablet. Once they got past Poughkeepsie and reached the foothills of the Adirondacks, the signal dropped completely.

"I can't get any baseball scores," he complained, shaking the tablet repeatedly in frustration. A thick binder rested on his lap and a stack of books on baseball analytics and statistics filled the seat beside him. "The Yankees are down by a run in the eighth with runners on second and third and no outs. And Barrett is pitching a no-hitter through six innings for the

White Sox in Cleveland. How am I going to know what happened and get all the stats to update my blog?"

"Sorry, sport," his father said from behind the wheel. "That's how it is out here in the boonies."

His mother turned around from the passenger seat to look at him. "Jake, remember that summer we lived outside Papillion in

Nebraska when your father was playing for the Storm Chasers? We could only get one AM radio station the entire summer."

"I was four years old then. I didn't know any better."

She smiled in recollection. "You had a lot of fun then. And once we get to Pine Barrows, you'll find plenty of fun things to do. You'll see."

Jake struck the tablet with the back of his hand in anger.

"You break that device, sporto, it's not going to be replaced," his father warned. "You won't be able to watch another game for a lot longer than the summer."

"Sorry," Jake muttered.

"You are my sunshine, my only sunshine," his mother began to sing from the front seat.

"Mom, I'm not a baby anymore."

When Jake was little and became upset, she would sing this song to him and it always calmed him down.

He held his fingers to his ears, but he could still hear her.

"You make me happy, when skies are gray," she continued. "You'll never know dear, how much I love you. So please, don't take my sunshine away."

She looked at Jake and smiled. He couldn't help smiling back as he removed his fingers from his ears.

Erin Lupo was tall, as far as mom's go, and pretty. Everyone who met her would tell his dad that she was enchanting or "a sight" or something like that, and Jake thought so too.

"When we get there, we should have better reception," she told him. "Don't worry. Okay?"

"Okay, Mom."

She always knew just what to say to make him feel better about whatever was troubling him, whether it was getting a bad grade at school or anxiety about moving to new place.

Still, Jake was not happy about being electronically disconnected from the world of baseball. Looking up from his device for the first time since they left the city, he noticed that there were no other cars in sight. They were on a two-lane road in the middle of the country, with nothing but woods all around. He stared out the window, transfixed by the trees passing by his field of vision in a blur. The motion made him drowsy, and he soon began to drift off. He was almost asleep when garbled voices brought him back to full alertness. He thought it was his mother or father calling him, but they were staring straight ahead in silence. The talking continued. The speech was mostly gibberish, but he listened closely and some of the words became decipherable.

He's here. Jake has arrived. Welcome, Jake.

It was not a single individual speaking, but a multitude, with more than one often talking at the same time. As the voices grew more intense, Jake once more pressed his fingers against his ears, again to no avail.

At long last. We've been waiting for you. We can even the score now.

At the same time, he closed his eyes tightly, as if to squeeze the voices out of head. It seemed to work, and when he opened them a moment later the voices were gone. However, he was stunned by what he saw as he looked out at the dense forest. His vision was keen. He was able to peer deeper into woods and he could see everything in great detail; expansive areas of fallen trees, outcroppings of rock, and an array of wildlife. Animals ranging in size from deer and black bears to chipmunks and squirrels scurrying around on the forest floor. In the canopies of trees were every species of native birds, and even a white owl alighted on the branch of a scarred leafless oak.

More and more forest life came into view. It was like looking at one of those Magic Eye 3D posters that, if you stare at long enough, a hidden image pops out at you.

He began to see people. At least that's what he thought at first. They were all different shapes and sizes, though not like adults and children. In fact, not really human at all. Some were quite small and others extremely large. Their bodies had peculiar physical traits. Some had limbs of animals, antlers and tails. Their faces were just as odd, featuring long noses and pointy ears.

Jake thought his eyes were playing tricks on him, and that these were just campers whose true appearances were being distorted by their distance from him and the speed the car was traveling, his mind confusing the shapes of their bodies with the arrangement of rocks and boulders, mistaking their facial features with surrounding trees and vegetation. He blinked several times to regain his focus, but he could still see them, milling around in the woods, dancing, playing strange games.

The front of the car dipped suddenly and sprang back up violently, bouncing everyone around inside. Jake struck his head on the roof. His mother let out a soft scream.

"Whoa! Sorry," his father apologized. "I didn't see it in time. Everyone ok? Erin? Jake?"

"I'm fine," his mother responded.

"Me, too. What was that?" Jake asked, picking his books up off the floor.

"Pothole," his mother said. "It sure came out of nowhere."

"We're officially off the grid," his father declared. "Rural roads like this don't get the attention they deserve. That's something else we have to get used to out here."

"We're getting close," his mother proclaimed.

"How do you know?" Jake asked. "We don't even have GPS out here."

"We still have this." His mother unfolded a large, creased map. A fluorescent yellow Hi-Liter pen traced their journey from Brooklyn to Pine Barrows. "This was how we used to get to places before society became so dependent on technology."

"Hey, Jake, see that hill up ahead?" His father pointed out the front windshield at a long grass-covered mound in the distance that rose to considerable height. "That's how Pine Barrows got its name. A barrow is a large mound of earth or stones. I looked on-line to find out all I could about the town. I didn't find much, but one article suggested that the mound could be ancient Indian burial site, or perhaps the final resting place of Civil War soldiers. Isn't that interesting?"

"Slow down a little," his mother suggested. "Our street is right off this road. It should be coming up. We have to keep our eyes open. Watch out!" she suddenly shouted.

His father swerved to avoid several potholes this time. "I've never seen roads this bad," he exclaimed.

Jake glanced out the window and was amazed by what he saw. There were more holes than road. His father had to carefully navigate around all the debris as well as the potholes. There were scatterings of broken glass, chunks of Fiberglass and larger recognizable automobile parts such as wiper blades, mufflers, and a bunch of hubcaps. "Holy crow! Look at the size of that one." He marveled at a pothole he imagined may have been made by the impact of a small meteor.

Suddenly, from the middle of the mini crater, a small pickax, gripped by two dirty hands, flashed upward, halted momentarily, then pitched downward and out of sight. Jake pressed his face against the glass to get a better look. He thought it might be a construction worker repairing the road, but whoever it was seemed to be dutifully employed in digging rather than mending the hole. The violent motion was repeated, and every time the tool struck the rocky gravel beneath the street, some of the dirt kicked up and landed on the surface of the road.

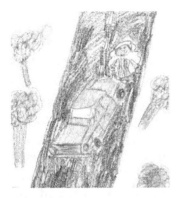

With his father driving slowly, Jake was able to see directly inside the massive pothole. The first thing he realized was that it was not nearly as deep as he thought. The more striking observation was that the digger was torturously small, although his hands and bare feet were oversized. The creature was pear-shaped and had a protruding belly. Its spindly arms were corded with bulging veins and sinewy muscle. The three-cornered hat it wore had holes cut into the rim to allow its large ears to protrude.

As the car passed, the digger stopped what it was doing and stood stiffly in place. It turned his bulbous head and looked directly at Jake, eyes wide with surprise. It had a thin, pointed nose, like the end of a broom handle. Shaggy tufts of curly brown hair fluttered from its bare torso as its chest contracted from the heavy labor. The only piece of clothing on its body was a pleated wool cloth that covered it from its midsection to its knees, held up by a strap that went over one shoulder.

Jake closed his eyes and reopened them, but he could still see the little man glaring at him. His parents gave no indication that they saw it. The startled expression on the little man's face did not change as its eyes followed the departing vehicle.

It was a goblin.

Jake waved and the goblin waved back.

As the goblin in the pothole faded into the distance, a sign carved into the trunk of a large tree proclaimed, WELCOME TO PINE BARROWS. Fresh, golden brown sap filled the engraved letters and dripped down the bark.

"There it is," his mother announced.

A rusted metal sign attached to a weathered wooden post read, TISDALE ROAD. They traveled down a narrow dirt lane lined on both sides by tall trees whose thick canopies converged, blotting out almost all of the sunlight. His father had to put on the headlights in order to see where he was going. They drove that way for a few minutes before they rounded a turn and could see light at the end of the forested tunnel. The woods suddenly dissolved and they emerged into an immense open expanse, squinting from the bright sunshine. It looked as if a section of land had been gouged out of the dense woodland. A two-story farmhouse sat smack in the middle of several acres of clear-cut land, surrounded on all sides by thousands of acres of raw, untouched wilderness. There was a large pond at the edge of the property, most of the water contained within the woods, all of it gone to swamp.

It was just as it had been described in the realty ad: *If you have ever wanted to escape the everyday grind to be in a place that you can see and feel nature all around you, this is the place.*

Jake thought it should have mentioned something about the goblins that lived there, but he understood why they left that out.

Gravel crunched under the tires as the car came to a stop in the circular driveway near the front of the Lupo's new home. The original farmhouse was built in the 1600s, having undergone many restorations over the centuries. While it may have been sufficiently modernized over the many years, it was in need of additional renovations. The front porch was sagging, and chips of white exterior paint were curled up on the outside walls or lying on the ground like the house was molting.

His parents '*ooh-ed*' and '*aah-ed*' as they got out to inspect the lay of the land around the farmhouse and to peer out at the grand views of the rolling valleys and the surrounding mountains in the distance.

Jake stayed behind to collect his baseball books, which he did not allow to be shipped ahead of time with everything else. They filled the entire trunk as well as the back seat.

The virtual silence in the country was overwhelmed by the voices that continued to call out to him inside his head.

Bottom of the 1st

In front of three twisted thorn trees growing close together, a frightful creature paced back and forth. The goblin Overlord was tall and covered with short, matted black hair. He resembled a black devil with long goat ears and burning red eyes. Buach's long, heavy tail slithered behind him, tearing the underbrush and raking the soil as he moved along the ground. His impatience grew as he awaited the arrival of his Underlord.

The arrangement of the enchanted thorn trees disguised the secret entrance of Buach's fortress, concealing it not only from humans but from his most loyal disciples, including his Underlord. He did not have sentries or personal guards because he did not trust anyone, and he was determined to keep his lair camouflaged until after his power became supreme, which could only happen when the Sacred Amulet was in his possession. It required a great deal of his power to conceal his fortress from sight, that's why finding the Sacred Amulet was so important.

Buach peered menacingly into the forest for any sign of his Underlord. The other mythical inhabitants of Pine Barrows who were lurking nearby in the cold darkness of the woodlands stirred anxiously in Buach's presence. The Overlord's power instilled great fear in the goblin community, and he reveled in their trepidation and cowering respect.The number of dryads and assortment of tree nymphs that had once inhabited these woods had depleted significantly, fleeing in great numbers since their queen died and Buach established The Order, seizing control of the goblin kingdom. All that remained to oppose Buach and his evil followers were the goblins of the Resistance, who were determined to hold onto their kingdom and continue playing the game of baseball.

Both sides, the Order and the Resistance, had goblins who were not what they appeared, working for the other side as informants. Buach didn't know who might be just a sympathizer to the opposition's cause or who was a secret member of the Resistance plotting against him, but his deep suspicion of everyone was reflected in his paranoia.

Buach snorted in exasperation over his Underlord's delay, a low droning howl that sent many fabled woodland beings scattering into the safety of the dense canopy above and under the thick underbrush on the forest floor.

Sensing movement under its cloven feet, the beast stopped suddenly and bent over to inspect the ground underfoot. Nostrils flaring, Buach kicked over a decaying clump of leaves to expose a thick worm burrowing into the earth. In an instant, a long purple tongue extended out of the goblin's mouth and ripped the worm from the soil. Before the slimy nematode even knew what happened, it disappeared down the Overlord's gullet as a snack.

Buach raised his head upon hearing the approach of his Underlord. It was a sound that could only be made by a fachan.

Few monsters of folklore were more dreadful in appearance than this malformed, nightmarish brute which possessed a single set of body parts, most prominent being its thickly muscled leg covered in mangy fur and feathers. The face of this monstrosity featured a giant solitary eye and a wide, broad mouth that contained a black, pointy tooth. A rigid strand of hair stuck straight up like a horn on the top of its head. A hand with fingers like talons protruded from the center of its leg-body. Standing a formidable eight feet tall, it hopped along on its mighty leg, the ground shuddering as the thing advanced. A long club with a head made of flanged bone was fastened to its side by a cowhide belt.

"Peg Leg Jack," Buach snarled. "It's about time. I've been waiting a human's lifetime for your arrival."

Garbhan did not like being called Peg Leg Jack, but only Buach could get away with it. Anybody else he would strike down with his mace without hesitation.

"Sorry, my Lord," the cyclops apologized. "I came as soon as I could. The entrance to your fortress is hidden."

"Of course, it is hidden," Buach roared. "I would be a sitting duck if it was visible."

"I didn't know where you would appear, that's why it took me so long to find you?"

"Never mind your oafish excuses, Peg Leg Jack. It was *you* who summoned *me*. Just tell me what you have learned."

"Well, not only are the members of the Resistance continuing to play baseball, but they have recruited a human to play for them."

Buach drew in a deep breath before exhaling sharply. "A human?"

"Yes. He arrived today with his family, a woman and a boy."

"They are here in Pine Barrows?" the Overlord bellowed. "And they were not stopped? A human family settles into our kingdom and you do nothing? As second-in-command, one of your duties is to keep your eye open for outsiders and do what needs to be done to keep them out. I should have you demoted or banished for incompetence."

Buach's voice rose with each pronouncement and the fachan took a half-hop backward, shuddering his eye in anticipation of a violent blow from an angry Buach. Instead, he got another question.

"Where are they now?"

"They are staying at the Tisdale folk house."

"Blackburn," Buach mumbled accusatorily. "He's helping them. But why?"

"I don't know, Sire."

"I know you don't know, you fool. I wasn't asking you."

Garbhan's eyeball rolled around in all directions. "Who are you asking then? There's no one else here, is there?"

"It's rhetorical."

"What? *Historical*?"

"Never mind. We need to find out one thing; why did Blackburn bring the human here?" He scowled at the fachan.

"Is that question for me?" Garbhan asked tentatively. "Or is it historical?"

"I hope you have more to report to me, Peg Leg Jack. For your sake."

"I do." Garbhan's words were measured. "Lorcan informed me that the human boy observed him. And waved at him."

Buach's eyes burned red, emitting heat and smoke from an internal fire. "What was Lorcan doing when he was seen by the human?"

"Searching for the Sacred Amulet, Sire. He was in Ruadhan's dig crew near the Tisdale folk house. Lorcan was taken into custody the moment Ruadhan observed the sighting by the human boy. I interrogated Lorcan myself. I did not go easy on him."

"Was Lorcan not provided with sufficient magic to render himself invisible to human eyes? Or did he use the power for some other purpose?"

"He told me he used all of the magic for concealment."

"Bah! He cannot be trusted," Buach ranted. "How can any goblin among you be trusted?"

"Lorcan also reported that only the boy had seen him, not the other humans."

Buach's breath caught deep in his throat as he carefully considering what Garbhan revealed. "Many human children possess the ability to perceive our world, a talent that will leave them as they grow into adulthood, with most never knowing they had it. So, the fact that the boy saw Lorcan is not that unusual. But for this to be happening at this time is a problem. This family must be forced to leave Pine Barrows as soon as possible. Until I figure out what to do, we will have to be careful around the boy. For now, make sure the others keep their distance from him."

The fachan nodded vigorously, the movement of his head causing him to hop up and down on his leg.

"I'd still like to know what Blackburn has in mind. That troublesome coach of the Mountain Men has some plan hatched. See what you can find out."

"What would you like to be done with Lorcan?" Garbhan answered his own inquiry in his next breath. "Have him destroyed; I should think." The fachan's eye blinked incessantly as he waited for a response. "You are wise not to trust him."

"No. The hogboon is the only one who has rightful access to the folk house. He will be needed to search the premises for the Sacred Amulet. It must be there. It has not turned up anywhere else."

"Sire, *any* goblin may enter the house, *if invited*," Garbhan offered. "It doesn't have to be Lorcan."

"The Sacred Amulet is well-hidden. And well-protected. We could use up all of our magic looking for it there and *still* not find it. Let Blackburn use up what little power the Resistance has to protect it. It will weaken their side and strengthen ours. Besides, Lorcan knows the house better than anyone. He will be the one to locate the Sacred Amulet for us."

"If it is even there," Garbhan pointed out. "Which it may not."

Buach's head snapped to attention and every muscle in his body became rigid with anticipation. "Is that a challenge?" he asked. His voice was almost joyous. "I say it is in the house. We have dug up nearly every inch of Pine Barrows and have turned up nothing. I accept your challenge. What shall we wager? You name it."

Garbhan gasped and slowly shook his head when he realized that his words had unintentionally triggered the Overlord's overriding sense of competition. Whenever Buach felt he was being challenged, he simply could not back down, no matter how slight the provocation or how high the stakes. This aggressive, risk-taking aspect of his personality had served him well so far, but it could just as well be his undoing, and his enemies knew it.

"No, your Lordship. I do not care to wager. I am in full agreement with you. You're right. It's probably there."

"It *must* be there. Or this will come back on you with devastating consequences. Locating the Sacred Amulet is your charge, and you have failed woefully. If it does not turn up in the folk house, you are of no further use to me."

"It will be found, my Overlord. I just need a little more time."

"Your time is all but up."

"I am being exceedingly thorough in my duties, which I take very seriously. Much of the wooded areas have been thoroughly searched, as you have observed. Only the soil beneath the paved roadway remains, and trows continue to dig all night in this quest. I can vouch that these creatures work extremely hard, but many of these road surfaces were laid directly over old railroad tracks, and the iron is making many of them ill, or killing them. They need stronger magic to protect them."

"I do not care about the trows," Buach fumed. "I cannot waste my powers on the likes of them." He leaned forward, pushing his face close to the fachan, who could feel the heat radiating from the Overlord's eyes. "Listen to me carefully, Peg Leg, Jack. I only chose you as my second-in-command because you are so repellant to look at, even to me. You have one use, and that is to find the Sacred Amulet. Finding it is all that matters. Do you understand?"

"Yes. I will see to it."

"You have said that before, and I am no closer to possessing the Sacred Amulet. Maybe I should make Ruadhan Underlord and hold you in captivity along with the others for not doing your job."

The fachan held its forked tongue. With Buach angered, Garbhan understood how much danger he was in at that moment. One slip-up could cost him his life.

"The longer the Resistance has hope, and as long as they continue to play baseball, we will not be able to defeat them. Now these humans must be dealt with. I will take care of them myself. That will eliminate whatever outside help that the

Resistance may have been counting on. And once the Sacred Amulet is my possession, I will crush the Resistance once and for all. When there are no goblins playing baseball in Pine Barrows, the power generated by the game will be short-circuited and I will become not just the ruler of this goblin kingdom, but Supreme Goblin Ruler. So, find the Sacred Amulet." Buach glared at his Underlord. "Go!"

"Yes, my Overlord."

From the distance came an unholy clamor as the woods filled with the sound and sight of a chicken stampede. On the backs of the farm animals were small green goblins. They had eyes the size of pepper seeds and elongated mouths filled with needle-sharp teeth. They whooped and hollered as they held the reigns in their three-fingered hands and dug their heels of their three-toed feet into the sides of the feathered beasts of burden. Hundreds of tiny demons on their poultry mounts gathered around Buach from three directions. This insane barnyard posse was of no tactical use to Buach. The Overlord only liked to have them around him because of their great number.

Garbhan detested the pesky things. They left behind chicken droppings that he was always stepping in. He wanted to swat them away like so many gadflies, but Buach's power and influence restrained him from acting on this impulse.

Buach turned and stalked away, his tail cutting a swatch through the underbrush.

The fachan watched the Overlord as he and his horde of Kallikantzaros marched off behind him. His unblinking yellow eye followed Buach until he disappeared into the shadows. Only when they were out of view did Garbhan pivot on his thick heel and stomp off, muttering to himself as he smashed pellets left by the chickens under his colossal foot.

Ruadhan, a shapeshifting hobgoblin known as a pooka, was in the form of a mountain hare. He was crouched in the underbrush, listening and scheming. This was his opportunity to make a name for himself and rise up in rank within the Order. Buach was clearly not happy with his Underlord, so the time was right to show the Overlord that he was more worthy of the position than Garbhan, who couldn't even shapeshift. Ruadhan already had a plan worked out to oust the fachan and take his place. Lorcan was the key, and when Buach found out what he did, he would have to be rewarded for his initiative, for achieving what Garbhan could not. How could Buach not instantly move him up to the number-two spot afterward?

Ruadhan took the form of an eagle and flew off to implement his plan. He searched the woods for the friendly hogboon who would assist him.

Top of the 2nd

Jake dragged himself out of bed. He hadn't slept well because of the persistent voices, though they diminished just before dawn. It helped when he turned on a small battery-operated transistor radio he had since they lived in Nebraska. It couldn't pick up any stations, but the static was enough to dull the chatter in his head.

He came downstairs wearing a baseball cap and carrying his glove and a thick spiral notebook. His mother greeted him with a smile and a kiss on the cheek as she put down a bowl of his favorite cereal. Grand Slam Crunch had oat flakes in the shape of baseball bats and tiny marshmallow baseballs. He pulled out a chair and sat down at the kitchen table, placing his glove and notebook beside the bowl. His mother fixed her eyes on him. Her silent stare prompted him to remove the glove and drop it onto the floor at his feet.

"How'd you sleep?" she asked.

"Good," he said. He didn't want to tell her about the voices. Like the goblin he'd seen in the pothole, she would just tell him it was his imagination. For Jake, that had always been an acceptable explanation, but seeing goblins and hearing them were two different things. They had never spoken to him before, and he didn't know why they would start now. "Did dad leave for practice yet?"

"He's getting his stuff ready. Someone's going to come by and pick him up in a bit."

"Did you find a way to get us connected to the rest of civilization?" Jake asked, his voice rising in hopeful anticipation.

His mother smiled sympathetically as she placed some milk and apple juice on the table in front of him. "It doesn't look good, honey. I think we're going to have to do without technology for a while."

"What? No way!"

"The only thing that works is an old land line phone," she informed him. "The wires must be underground. The residents of Pine Barrows probably don't want to have communications towers destroying the beauty of the land."

"What residents? Even Dad's coach, who supposedly lives on this street, is miles away."

"Well, I don't know how long we're going to be here, but we're all just going to have to make the best of it for a while. Oh, and I found these." She gestured to the countertop beside her.

"Walkie-talkies?" Jake jumped up to inspect the pair. "Cool."

"I thought you'd like them. They're real antiques. I'm surprised they still work."

They were big and heavy. Jake knew how to operate them. He had a toy set when he was younger. He turned them both on, producing a high-pitched shrill that startled him. He quickly lowered the volume.

"Maybe later, after I unpack and get things straightened out a little around here, I can go out with you and we can explore. What do you say?" She grabbed one of the walkie-talkies and held it to her mouth. "Over."

"I have to throw my fifty pitches."

"Roger that." She knew that Jake's daily routine of throwing the pitches and logging the percentage of strikes in his notebook took precedence over everything else. "I'll have my ears on. You can contact me when you're done. Over and out."

Jake choked down his cereal and chugged the juice. His mother told him to slow down as he jumped up and placed the empty bowl and glass in the sink.

"I'll be outside," he said as he grabbed his glove, notebook, and a walkie-talkie and walked out the back door. The voices, though they remained faint and indiscernible, ticked up a notch. He imagined it was the buzz from a large crowd in a baseball stadium cheering him on as he made his way to the pitching mound. Back behind the farmhouse, there was a bucket of baseballs sixty feet away from where an old car tire was hanging from the limb of a maple tree. Jake took the tire with him wherever they traveled. His father had put it up soon after they arrived the day before.

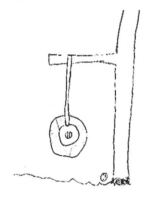

Throwing baseballs through a tire was what his father had done when he was a kid. Practicing every day helped him develop accuracy and arm strength, so Jake did the same thing. He threw fifty pitches each and every day, with the goal of throwing as many baseballs through the tire as he could. The most had ever gotten was forty-four out of fifty, and nineteen in a row was a personal best.

Now, he pretended that he was pitching in Game 7 of the World Series. Before each pitch, he made sure he took a deep breath, like his father taught him. When he got to his fiftieth and final pitch, he had already thrown a forty-five strikes, a new record. Inhaling and exhaling a final time, he went into his wind up and released the ball. It sailed straight through the center of the tire.

46

"Steeeeeeeeee-rike," his dad called out like a Major League umpire. Jake turned around and saw his father with a glove in one hand and a ball in the other. "Looking good, son. Fastball is really coming along. How about a little catch before I leave?"

"Sure."

They tossed the ball around in silence for a few minutes.

"So, Dad, are you nervous about the tryout? I would be."

"No, I'm not nervous. I'm lucky. Not only do I have a family that believes in me, but so does my new manager. He really loves baseball, too, I can tell. If he didn't, that would make me nervous. You can't trust a guy who doesn't like baseball."

"Hey, Dad, you want to see my curveball?"

"Sure. Let her rip."

Jake manipulated his fingers on the ball, his tongue peeking out of the corner of his mouth, took a deep breath, and then delivered a pitch that broke so much his father started to move to go get the ball before it sliced back to where he had been standing.

"Wow, Jake! That was the best one yet." His father walked over and gripped him around shoulder, pulling him close. "You know, I think it's time for you showcase that talent. They love their baseball here. I'll bet they have a local youth league you can play on."

"I don't think so."

"Why not? You're really good."

Jake looked down at his sneakers. "No, I'm not."

His father stooped over and gently lifted Jake's chin so they were eye to eye. "Look, I'll make a deal with you. If I make the Mound Men, you have to play. Deal?"

Suddenly a car horn blared at the front of the house. "That's them," his father said. He tossed the ball up for Jake, who caught it with his bare hand. "Wish me luck."

"You don't need luck, Dad. You'll be great."

"Thanks, sport. We'll talk more about this later." He gave his son a hug and jogged off with his glove on his hand like he was headed out to the mound from the bullpen.

Jake collected the baseballs he'd tossed through the tire and dropped them into the bucket. Most were just a few feet in the woods. He spotted one farther away, resting near a pile of wood. The pieces were neatly cut into six-foot lengths and the edges were notched. He grabbed one, and although the log appeared solid, he discovered that it was light enough to lift with one hand. They were all like that. The thought to build a fort occurred to him and he felt compelled to act on the impulse. He didn't really want to build it in the woods, but he figured that a fort was meant to be a secret and you couldn't have it out in the open where everyone could see it.

He searched for a good spot as close to the property line as possible, but that was no easy task. The woodlands all around the farmhouse were pockmarked with holes. There was a flat spot the right size about fifty yards in, and he carried the logs over to the site to build Fort Lupo. In no time, a six-foot square fort was complete. There was enough wood to cover the top and form a flat roof. He positioned one wall over the middle of a hole to allow access inside.

"Not bad," Jake told himself as he stood back to admire his handiwork. Just then he noticed that the bark of several nearby trees was coated with a glaze of thick sap. It was black where it was dry, and golden brown where it oozed from the trunk. This gave him another thought. He picked up a thick twig and pushed one end into a blob of sap, twirling the sticky material around on one end like a honey dripper. He carried it over to the fort and smeared the goop in a section between two logs. It formed an instant seal, and as he continued to plug the gaps in the wood, the sap oozed out of the tree more freely, as if to keep up with the demand. It was messy work, but it spread easily and dried quickly, and when he was done the fort was much sturdier.

He considered going to the house to bring back some packing blankets and a flashlight for the fort, but he wanted to go inside and check it out first. He grabbed a hold of his glove and his walkie-talkie and got down on his hands and knees. He crawled down into the hole, under the section of wall, and up into the fort on the other side.

Two things struck Jake the moment he entered the mini

shelter, the first being the absolute darkness and the other was the complete silence. The voices in his head stopped at once while the walls of the fort seemed to dissolve. He blindly pressed the speaker button on his walkie-talkie multiple times, but it wasn't working. He dropped the useless device. To reassure himself that he was still enclosed in the wood and sap fortress, he reached out to touch the sides, but even as he extended his arms as far as he could there was nothing in any direction. He raised his gloved hand above his head and slowly stood. Incredibly, there was no roof, either. He took a couple short, hesitant steps forward with his arms stretched out in front of him. He met no resistance and continued. He covered nearly twenty feet before he encountered a wall, not of wood but of dirt. He ran his hand along the cool, damp earth, keeping it at arm's length as he followed it forward in one direction, hoping it would lead him out of there.

In the distance there was a faint flicker of light. He followed the glow, and as he drew closer it illuminated enough for him to realize he was in a tunnel. Along the way, he observed several unlit torches on wall. The one burning ahead seemed to have been lit especially for him. When he reached it, the tunnel dead-ended and he stood before a large wooden door with no handle. He pushed on it and it swung inward slowly. Bright white light instantly flooded the dark tunnel, temporarily blinding him. He had to look away while his eyes adjusted. When he was able to turn back, through squinted eyelids, he found himself inside a dugout. Before him, under a dome of golden sunshine, was a baseball field with the greenest grass he had ever seen, contrasted against a perfectly manicured dirt infield diamond. There was a game going on, only the players were goblins. All but one. His father was on the mound.

"I see you brought your glove," said a gruff voice from the other end of the dugout. "If you had gotten here sooner, I could have put you in for an inning."

Jake turned and saw a wizened goblin wearing a baseball uniform and pacing back and forth.

"Jumping Joe Dugan!" Jake said breathlessly. "I knew you guys were real. I just knew it. It's not just my imagination. This is real. I always believed that magic existed."

"Your dad sure has magic in his right arm," the goblin manager said without diverting his attention away from the game.

"What is all this?" Jake inquired. "How did I get here?"

The goblin manager looked around at Jake momentarily. "I was expecting you. Hang on a minute, the game is about to end." Turning back to the field, the goblin manager cupped one bony hand against the side of his mouth. "One more, Lupo," he yelled. "Go right at him."

Jake scratched his head. *Expecting me?* he thought. *How could he be expecting me?*

The manager was no more than three feet tall, and despite head and facial features that were large for his body, he looked entirely human.

The two of them watched as his dad delivered a nasty slider that the goblin batter swung and missed. A big WHOOSHING sound was followed by the goblin umpire calling a third strike, ending the game.

"Great game, Lupo," the manager yelled. Leaning over to Jake, he said, "Recorded nine outs. No hits. No walks. Six strike outs. Thirty-five pitches. Put that in your book."

Jake's father was congratulated by his goblin teammates as he walked off the field and into the dugout. Jake took a couple steps backwards as the goblin players walked past him, some acknowledging him with a nod or a wink. A couple of them playfully pulled down on the bill of his cap. While relatively human-like, the variety in the size, shape and colors of the goblins astounded him. Some were very hairy, others completely bald. His father approached, collecting high fives and pats on the back. One of them followed closely behind his father, giggling as he gathered used bubblegum from his teammates and proceeded to gently stick the wet, pink gobs to the back of his father's cap. Jake's face lit up as his father approached, but his father walked right past him and stopped beside the manager.

"Excellent job, Lupo," the manager told him. "That was quite a debut. Your stuff was sensational. They couldn't touch you. How's the shoulder holding up?"

"Feels really good. It's great to be back out there. I really appreciate all you're doing for me and my family. I won't let you down."

"Glad to have you aboard. Go home and get some rest. And get that bubblegum off your cap. See you tomorrow."

His father removed his hat and smiled when he saw the wad of gum. He looked around and quickly found the offending goblin, who laughed heartily. "Prank," his father said, shaking his head good-naturedly.

"I got you, rookie," Prank snorted.

The other players hooted and cackled as they emptied down the tunnel at the other end of the dugout and headed to the clubhouse, leaving Jake and the manager alone.

"Skip Blackburn," the goblin said. He grasped Jake's hand and shook it vigorously. "I'm the manager of this club as you probably already guessed. You can call me Skip."

"Nice to meet you, Skip. Why didn't my father even look at me?"

"He can't see you," Skip told him. "He doesn't see his teammates as they really are, either. He sees them as human. It's a simple goblin spell. Magic."

"How come I can see them?"

"I'm sure you've been seeing our kind your whole life. You have a special ability, and we need you to help us. That's why you're here."

This instantly brought to Jake's mind some of the things that the voices in his head had been saying. *We've been waiting for you. We can even the score now.* "I don't understand, Skip."

The goblin manager took a deep breath. "Well, let me start by explaining that Pine Barrows is a unique and wonderous place. It's not at all as it appears to most humans. It's a kingdom that is cut off from the rule of the Goblin Court, sort of the badlands of the Goblin Realm. The inhabitants of these vast hills and woodlands are under the control of a troop of evil goblins who call themselves the Order, headed by Buach, the most evil goblin of all. He is to be rightfully feared. Those who did not safely flee Pine Barrows have been forced to do his bidding, or have otherwise subjected to his wrath, punished with imprisonment or worse. Many of those who have resisted have never been seen again."

"Has Buach always ruled Pine Barrows?"

"No. Our queen, who ruled this region for millennia, unexpectantly died recently. Goblins are magical beings who live a long time, and the death of a goblin queen is a rare occurrence, indeed. In the power vacuum that followed her death, while the rest of us mourned our beloved queen, Buach acted swiftly to seize control before he could be opposed. One of the ways Buach is attempting to consolidate his power is to banish goblins from playing baseball."

"He wants to banish baseball? But why? My dad always says that you can't trust anyone who doesn't like baseball."

"Your father is right about that. But Buach doesn't dislike baseball. Like all goblins, he loves to play. Many years ago, I was the coach of a team that he very badly wanted to make. He tried out, and I cut him. He became angry, and he has never gotten over it. Over the years, his anger festered and grew, and he became increasingly wicked and vile."

"So, he wants to banish goblins from playing baseball in Pine Barrows because he got cut from the team?"

"Partly. You see, to goblins, and many humans like you, baseball is more than just a game. It has a special power. You can feel it. Deep inside. It's magical. You know that feeling you get when you hit a ball so perfectly it doesn't seem to hit the bat. By banishing baseball, Buach aims to deprive Pine Barrows of that magic and harness its formidable power for his own sinister purpose of holding sway over the goblin kingdom."

"Can't he be stopped?"

"I'm afraid his simple plan to banish baseball is already in effect. But it's not complete. I am part of a group of goblins, the Resistance, who refuse to abandon Pine Barrows and give up baseball. If we stop playing baseball, we automatically provide Buach with unstoppable power. That is why we must continue to play, and ultimately conquer Buach and the Order. This is something we need your help to achieve. It is why you have been summoned to Pine Barrows."

"*Me*? What can I do?"

"You have a great power of which you are not aware." Skip spoke softly. He raised his chin and peered directly into Jake's eyes. "You see, my boy, in your veins you have goblin blood, which was contributed to you from *both* your parents. That is something that few humans possess. There are some humans with goblin DNA handed down from a distant relative, once in a while even a parent, but almost never both parents. That is what makes you so special."

"Do you mean that my parents are goblins?"

"Not exactly, my boy Your father has more goblin DNA in his blood than your mother, which is not surprising. Most Major League players have some degree of goblin blood in their veins. Because of your hereditary, you are what is known as an *otherkin*, and that is a source of great power, in both the human and the goblin world."

"Are my parents aware of any of this?"

"Not likely. When they were young children, they may have had visions or even encounters with goblins which they simply passed off as fanciful imaginings. The ability to observe goblins diminishes as humans age. And you must not whisper a word of this to them or any human, or you will put us all in greater peril. Promise?"

"I promise."

"Good. Now, at this moment anyway, Buach is not aware that you are an otherkin, or that I brought you here to help the Resistance. However, once he learns of this and your abilities, he will do whatever it takes to prevent you from wielding your power against him. Right now, the Order is desperately searching for the Sacred Amulet, an object of infinite power, and if Buach finds it, there will be no way to stop him. We are running out of time, and you're our only hope."

Jake took a half step back, as if to get a better perspective on everything he had seen and heard in the last few minutes. He had gone from seeing an occasional goblin in the woods or park to talking with one and discovering that he was somehow related to them. "I have a lot of questions," he said.

Storm clouds rapidly filled the sky, which darkened almost instantly. Shadows fell across Skip's face, his eyes wide and his mouth agape in terror. "You are in danger," he cautioned. "The Order and its forces are near. I do not have sufficient power to protect you.

You must go." Skip dragged Jake toward the wooden door at the end of the dugout with more strength than the boy thought the little fellow possessed.

"Can I contact you again?"

"You can reach me anytime through the portal you constructed from the wood of the magical Rowan tree. But I must warn you, it can be dangerous to do so. A goblin from the Resistance has been assigned to assist you. Be careful. Buach will dispatch evil goblins from the Order to confuse you and trick you into believing that they are your friends."

"Wait," Jake protested. "How will I know if they are with the Resistance or the Order?"

"Go." Skip shoved him hard through the doorway. Jake could not keep his feet underneath him and he tumbled headlong. He landed on his belly, the side of his head impacting the earthen floor hard enough to disorient him. For a long moment, he thought he might pass out, and he fought hard against it.

He was in complete darkness again.

Bottom of the 2nd

The pooka's golden, luminous eyes studied the hogboon's every movement from the safety of the forest. The shapeshifting goblin was in a chimeric form, part human but having the face of a goat, spiral horns, and hoofed feet. Ruadhan stayed out of view just inside a stand of trees that lined the edge of the woods on the west side of the Tisdale folk house.

Lorcan was small, but he was strong for his size, and he had no problem making it across the open expanse toward the forest carrying the human woman over his shoulders. She was not moving. She was enchanted, and in a deep sleep.

"Over here," Ruadhan called out. He tossed a large field stone in Lorcan's direction and hopped out from behind a twenty-foot alder tree, revealing his location by waving his arms before retreating into the welcoming darkness.

The hogboon spotted Ruadhan and headed over in that direction, stopping beside the pooka, who inspected the woman. Ruadhan ran his thick-nailed fingers through the human's long, blond hair. Erin Lupo did not stir. He looked up to address

Lorcan. "Did you incite the magic exactly as I directed? She must sleep and wake with no memory of the abduction."

"Yes, yes. I did it just as you said."

"Good work, hogboon. Buach will be pleased. Go finish it, now." Leaning forward, he extended his taut, muscular arms to accept the prize that Lorcan had in his possession, but the hogboon hitched his shoulders, pulling the woman out of his reach.

Ruadhan's eyes blazed and he hissed, baring jagged little teeth. Although Lorcan was much smaller, he did not recoil at this display.

"You dare defy an agent of the great Buach, knowing you will be crushed beneath his feet like he has done to so many others before."

"I just want to know what will become of her."

"Why should her circumstance be of any concern to you? Buach does not answer to anyone, least of all a lowly hogboon like you."

"Our kind are forbidden from harming humans."

Ruadhan gazed at the hogboon and growled deep in his throat. "Buach can do whatever he wishes."

"You are not Buach."

"I am a general in the Order, so if you want to continue to live in Pine Barrows - indeed, continue to *live* at all - you will be a good soldier and hand the human over *right now*."

Lorcan turned his head fully to the right so that Ruadhan had a full view of the left side of his face. His cheek was red and bruised, his eye still swollen after Garbhan's recent interrogation of him about the human boy. "You can do whatever you want to me, but I must abide by the goblin code."

Ruadhan took a deep breath. "I will tell what will become of the human woman only so that you will rightfully cower before Buach and the Order. The woman will enter the

Goblin realm and become a handmaiden in the new goblin court formed by Buach. Now hand her over."

Lorcan hesitated, then extended his arms to allow Ruadhan to reach down and take the human woman from him.

"Now go and finish the task, hogboon," the pooka commanded. "Put a fetch in her place. GO!"

Lorcan resented the arrogant shapeshifter for the way he pushed other goblins around. It was bad enough for goblins to harm humans, but it was another thing for goblins to threaten and hurt other goblins. Buach did not hold the lives of his own kind sacred, and for Ruadhan, to serve on his side, made him just as bad. Or worse.

For all his malevolence, Buach would stand no chance of succeeding if not for goblins like Ruadhan and Garbhan, who become instruments of evil, their actions guided by an Overlord who wanted to oversee the destruction of Pine Barrows and all its goblin inhabitants.

Lorcan broke off a large branch from the alder and held it out for Ruadhan to enchant. Reciting an ancient incantation, the limb was empowered with the magic to deceive humans by taking on the appearance of the woman. When the spell wore off, the woman would appear to have died, and the other humans will bury the piece of wood in the ground without anyone suspecting that the woman was actually still alive, though living in the goblin world. And once that happened, the woman would never be able to return to human world.

Lorcan thought it was a mean trick to play on humans. He didn't like being a part of it, even though he knew if he didn't do it, Ruadhan would get someone else who would. He thought about this, and the role *he* was playing in the conquest of the goblins of Pine Barrows. After helping in the abduction of the human, was he really any better than Ruadhan? Both of them were just doing what they were told. What did it matter the reason? Whether his own motivation was fear and self-preservation rather than Ruadhan's desire to prop up Buach as the goblin ruler, the result was the same. He was still helping the Order destroy everything that the goblins in the kingdom held dear. He didn't know what to do. He was not a great thinker, but he did not feel good about what he had done.

"Quickly, you fool," Ruadhan compelled the hogboon.

Lorcan sighed as he walked up the front porch of the folk house and placed the enchanted branch on the worn wooden chair beside the front door. It was full dusk as he stepped back down onto the lawn.

What have I done, Lorcan thought as he looked up at the edge of the woods where the outline of a sleek, dark horse with a long, flowing mane and luminous yellow eyes pierced the darkness? With the unconscious woman on the back of the nightmare steed, Ruadhan rode off like a thunder bolt into the depths of the forest. By the time Lorcan reached the woods, the shapeshifting pooka was long gone.

It was not the weight of the woman bearing down on Ruadhan that drained him. Considerable energy radiated from her in waves, causing the hairs of his black mane to tingle. Without sufficient magic to suppress this force, he grew weak, his legs tiring with each stride he took. He had slowed considerably, with barely enough strength remaining to summon Buach. The woman's power was surprising, but it would have no effect on Buach and the vast power that he yielded. Ruadhan would be at the mercy of the Overlord's response.

Ruadhan did not see the twisted thorn trees, but when Buach materialized out of thin air, a shiver of fear prickled his equine flesh. The Overlord appeared alone, his freakish demon escorts nowhere in sight. His fiery eyes were already filled with great rage. Ruadhan expected Buach to become even angrier as he laid the woman gently on the ground. The pooka knew he would have to talk fast and make a convincing point that this unsanctioned maneuver was solely for the benefit of the Order, so he changed into an owl. He felt majestic and stately as he alighted on the branch of a nearby tree.

"Tell me what you have done?" the beast demanded.

"This is the woman from the folk house, O' Vile One."

"Why have you brought her here?"

"She is yours to do with as you desire, your Grand Wickedness."

"Umm," he muddled. "Why is your breath so ragged, pooka?"

"It was a long journey, My Exalted Fetid Fiend. She is heavier than she looks. She's...um...solid."

"What am I to do with her?"

"She'd make an excellent handmaiden."

"I have no need for a handmaiden," Buach snapped. "I have Garbhan, you, and soon all of Pine Barrows to serve me."

"A queen, perhaps."

"Are you joking, pooka?" the Overlord's voice rose with his agitation. "I rule alone. A queen will eventually try to leech power from my hands and into her own. I did not sanction this abduction." He took a threatening step toward Ruadhan, rising on his haunches until he was towering over the shapeshifter. "Who told you to do this?" he screamed. "Was it Garbhan?"

"No, Professor of Putrefaction," Ruadhan began, cowering in fear. "I did it myself. I thought it would be beneficial to you."

As Buach's rage intensified, his dark body grew many shades blacker, making him all but imperceptible in the shaded backdrop of the surrounding forest. Only his blazing eyes could be seen. "No, you thought it would be beneficial to *you*," the Overlord said as he grasped the owl firmly in one hand and positioned a razor-sharp talon of his other hand close to an eye of the noble bird. "From the beginning, you have been working your way up the ranks to become my number-three, doing whatever it took to get ahead, while stepping over and on anyone who got in your way." Just as the body around his flaming eyes dissolved into pitch darkness, it suddenly began to lighten. "I like that," Buach said in approval, the edge in his voice softening. "You are trying to push out Garbhan and supplant him as my Underlord. I like that even better." He retracted the talon back slightly from the pooka's eye. "It is the kind of decisive action that can get you into the position of Underlord. It is also the kind that can get you killed."

Ruadhan saw his opportunity. "I thought that she, as a human, would be someone who could not be corrupted the way that a goblin would. Someone who, if you chose to be your queen, could provide you with offspring who would defend you, and who you could trust to take over the reins of power when you were ready to pass them, of course, rather than getting into frequent skirmishes with greedy, backstabbing goblins who seek to steal all that you have rightfully earned."

Buach fetched up at once. "Hmmm," he began, his body lightening further. "What you say makes sense, I will give you that." He glared intensely at the shapeshifter. "And there is nothing you seek for yourself?"

Ruadhan dodged the accusation like a dart. "I only want what is best for the Order, for your reign. And to rid the kingdom of baseball, which I loathe, as do you, Ruthless One."

Buach leered at him with fierce, calculating eyes. "I have long thought it wise to never trust a shapeshifter. I don't know that I should start now. There is too much at stake. I will let you live, but I will keep an eye on you." Glancing down at the sleeping woman, he sneered. "I haven't decided what to do with her yet, but perhaps she will be of some use."

"Yes, Maestro of Mayhem. She should provide a wealth of information when she awakes, which should not be long. Little magic was used, and when the fetch substituted for her withers and dies, the other humans should leave Pine Barrows forever, and never look back."

"Seems like you have thought of everything, pooka?"

"Only you can think of everything, *Herr* Ruler of Refuse. I was only thinking in the moment when this idea struck me to get rid of the humans, and the problems they may cause you."

"What 'problems' do you think these humans can cause for me?"

"Well, I-I didn't mean *problems*, exactly. That was a poor choice of words. Nuisance is what I meant. The humans could never be any kind of a problem for you."

Buach gently secured a single feather of the owl between two pincer-like fingers. With a swift tug, he plucked the feather from the body of the bird, which screeched in pain, the three lids of each eye closing simultaneously.

"Next time you're thinking about something, and you are struck with an idea, you better be sure you think of asking me before you take any action."

"Yes, yes, Kaiser of Cruelty. You can count on me."

"For your sake, I hope you are right." The Overlord held the feather in front of the bird's wide eyes. "Here. Hold onto this." Ruadhan grasped the feather between his toes. "And let it be a reminder to you what will happen should there be a *next time*. This will be the only feather you will have remaining. Now, fly away."

As Ruadhan soared off into the trees, he observed Buach scoop the human woman into his arms before disappearing.

Top of the 3rd

Jake looked up, momentarily disoriented. Though he could not see a thing, he knew he was back inside the fort. All he wanted to do was go home. He reached out to feel the walls of the enclosure around him. Behind him, a pool of faint light filled the hole under the wall. He searched along the ground with his hands until he found the walkie-talkie, then quickly scrambled outside, where diffuse light from the waxing moon drifted down through the treetops like ghostly snowflakes. Somehow, he had been gone much longer than he thought was possible.

"Mom! Mom, can you hear me? Mom!" he spoke urgently into the walkie-talkie, knowing his mother would be worried.

"You fetch, I fetch, you fetch, I fetch," a callous, unidentifiable voice gurgled and then laughed through the speaker.

Jake looked down at the transceiver as if it had been transformed into a snake. After a moment, he tentatively pressed the call button. "Mom?"

"You fetch, I fetch, you fetch, I fetch."

Whoever had the other walkie-talkie, it wasn't his mother. After everything that Skip told him, it was impossible for him not to think that his mother wasn't in grave danger. He ran toward the clearing and his house on legs that felt like they were filled with cement. As he approached the lightless porch, he saw a shadowy

figure of his mother sitting motionless on the swinging chair near the door. Her body was not solid, but ethereal, translucent.

"M-Mom?" The nearer he drew the more insubstantial she became. By the time he reached the front porch, she was gone. On the chair was a tree branch. Next to it was a walkie-talkie, humming softly in the "on" position.

The unit crackled to life. *"You fetch, I fetch, you fetch, I fetch,"* a tinny voice squawked.

Jake heard laughter in the distance and looked up at the foreboding woods. The ground around the farmhouse was bathed in the ambient light of a full moon, but the surrounding forest was veiled in darkness. Near the edge, the ghostly figure of his mother lingered. Her hair swayed gently along the sides of her face, as if underwater. She beckoned him, but as he stepped forward, she retreated into the woods, floating rather than walking. The faster he moved, the further away she got. He couldn't catch her. It was like chasing a rainbow.

"Mom, wait. Mom." He knew it was not his mother as he pursued the apparition into the woods, and he stopped when he realized how far he had gone. The clearing and farmhouse were barely visible behind him through the dense stand of trees.

Suddenly the sound of something moving through water drew his attention. The pond was a vast shadow before him, a flat, black silhouette that stretched outward like an obsidian lava field. A ripple broke the smooth surface as something unseen neared the edge. He thought it might be an alligator, and he would have retreated to a safer distance if he could move. He stood transfixed. It was almost at the shore before he got a good look at it. The first thing to emerge were two extremely long, algae-covered arms that resembled tree branches. Bobbing up out the water behind them, green and slimy, was a partially submerged face with black, deep-set eyes. Long hair, like seaweed, trailed behind.

"Who goes there?" the water-witch gurgled, speaking even as she drew water into her voluminous mouth. She reached the edge of the pond and slowly stood upright. The water was waist deep, her arms at her side, deep below the surface. Her wet hair hung down from her shoulders and covered most of her body. The flesh that was visible was bloated and waterlogged. She extended her lengthy arms out in front of her and plunged her crooked fingers into the muddy shoreline in front of Jake.

"Who are you?" he asked, trying to keep his voice as steady as possible. He didn't think he could have imagined anything as frightful in his worst nightmare.

"They call me Jenny Greenteeth," the hag answered, displaying a mouthful of teeth stained with moss. "Terrible name to call a woman as beautiful as me, don't you agree?"

"Do you know where my mother is?"

"I might," Jenny Greenteeth replied. "Come into the pond and I will tell you."

He took a step backward to be sure he was out of reach of the water witch's clawed hands that were submerged in the wet ground near his feet.

"There are all kinds of monstrous creatures lurking in these woods at night. You'll be safer in here with me. They all know not to mess with Jenny Greenteeth."

Leave now, while you can, a voice whispered in his head. There was a sense of urgency in the command, and he heeded the warning. He quickly turned and headed out of the woods.

"Where are you going?" Jenny snarled.

"To find my mother."

"Don't leave yet," the water-witch said, laughing. "I'm so hungry. I haven't eaten in so long. Come back and see me. I'll be waiting." Her laughter dissolved as she retreated back under the black surface of the pond, sound bubbles percolating up from the depths.

When Jake got back to the farmhouse, he saw that the porch light was on now and the walkie-talkie was still on the rocking chair. The stick was gone. He found it strange that there were also lights on inside the house. He paused a moment at front door, not knowing what to expect when he opened it. When he thought about what was waiting for him in the woods, he quickly stepped inside and shut the door behind him, the latch echoing around the quiet farmhouse. He proceeded through the entryway, past the empty kitchen, and into the unoccupied living room. The layout was completely unfamiliar to him. It felt like he was in someone else's house. Normally, when they moved somewhere, they took at least some of their stuff with them. The farmhouse was fully furnished. There was even food in the refrigerator when they arrived, all fresh, as well as dried and canned goods in the cupboards and pantry. They brought only clothes, most of which had been shipped out ahead of their drive to Pine Barrows.

When Jake reached the staircase, he saw his father's baseball bag near the landing. "Dad?"

"Jake," his father called down. "Up here."

Jake dashed up the stairs two at a time. The light was on in his parents' bedroom and he walked in to find his father standing over the bed where his mother was sitting up under the covers. She was holding a water globe in her hands. It was a gift from Aunt Briget. She sent it to them after finding out they were moving to the mountains. Inside the water-filled dome was an autumn forest setting with luminous gold flecks that drifted down on the trees when you shook it.

"What's going on?" Jake asked.

His father turned around to face him. "Your mother's not feeling well. I got home a few minutes ago and put her in bed."

"I'm fine," his mother insisted. "I'm just a little tired because I haven't really eaten all day. I got so caught up in straightening the house that I skipped lunch. And I promised to go outside with Jake, but time got away from me. Sorry, Jake."

Jake knew right away that this wasn't his mother. It looked exactly like her, but it was an imposter.

"That's okay." He hesitated, before adding, "Mom."

"There's really no need to make a big fuss," his mother said as she threw back the covers and got out of bed. "I'll feel better once I put something in my stomach."

"Are you sure, Erin?"

"Positive."

"Okay." His father took her by the hand and led her out of the room. "Let's all go down and I'll fix us something to eat." As he escorted her downstairs, she was smiling and giggling softly as she stared at the globe in her other hand, shaking it, and watching the shining gold flakes cascade down on the mini forest trapped under the glass.

"I bought some farm fresh vegetables and eggs from a roadside farmstand on the way home," his father announced when they got to the kitchen. "I can make a tasty zucchini omelet."

"That sounds delicious," his mother said. "But I don't think I can wait. I'm ravenous. I need to have a little snack first." As his father organized the kitchen, his mother went to the panty and opened a can of peaches. She started eating the contents with her fingers, licking the heavy syrup as it dripped down her hand.

His father laughed. "That Prank," he said.

Jake saw him holding all twelve eggs in one hand. As if by magic, he held them suspended above the carton. "He glued the eggs together."

"Who?" Jake asked.

"One of the guys on the team. Prank. He's always doing things like this. When I got to the clubhouse this morning, he had my locker filled with popcorn. When I opened it, the popcorn spilled all over the floor. Everyone enjoyed that one." His father shook his head and smiled as he pondered how he was going to break the glued-together eggs. "Jake, can you set the table?"

"Sure, Dad." He collected three dinner plates and silverware, placing a setting down in front of his mother, who was sitting at the kitchen table gorging herself on junk food. After she finished the peaches, she devoured half a bag of marshmallows and started on a sleeve of chocolate chip cookies. Jake had never seen his mother eat like that before. It was as if she hadn't eaten in a month, not just one afternoon.

"So how did it go today, Dad?" he asked as his father cooked.

"It went really well," his father said. "We had an intersquad game and I pitched the final three innings. My arm felt great, and I finished strong, striking out the last batter of the game.

"I know. I-I mean, I told you. I knew you we ready. Didn't I tell you, Dad?"

"You sure did."

"What about the players?" Jake asked. "What are they like?"

"An interesting group of guys. I'll put it that way. Like Prank. But you can tell they really love baseball. They have fun, but they are good, too. Early in the game today, our right fielder, Bud Willowbug, hit a homerun that struck the foul pole and snapped it in two. That's how hard he hit it."

"Whoa! Really?"

"It's true. We had to play the rest of the game with half a foul pole." He was still grinning as he brought the steaming pan of eggs loaded with vegetables over to the table and emptied them into a big platter. "What about you, sport? What did you do today?"

Jake told him about the fort he'd built from the pile of wood he found, but he stopped short of telling him that it somehow became a magic portal that transported him to a goblin world in which all three of them were inextricably tied. He wanted to tell his father about his belief that evil goblins did something with his real mother, but with her at the table, or whoever it was pretending to be her, he didn't want to give it away that he knew. Besides, he promised Skip he wouldn't breathe a word to anyone.

"My son, the engineer," his father said, and tousled Jake's hair. "I can't wait to see it. Well, everyone, dig in. Erin, do you want me to fix your plate?"

Her face was drawn and her eyelids were half closed. She sat very still, breathing shallowly, and looking off into the distance as if she could see through the kitchen wall. "I think maybe I do need to lie down for a little while after all," she mumbled, getting unsteadily to her feet. "I'm feeling really tired all of a sudden."

Jake's father helped her into the living room, placing a blanket over her as she settled in the recliner. "Take all the time you need," he said. "Just relax."

Jake watched through the open archway as his mother followed the flight of a ladybug around the room with giddy excitement. She squealed with delight when it landed on her shoulder and howled with laughter when it flew off toward the high ceiling near the front door. Then she closed her eyes and fell instantly asleep.

"What happened to Mom?" he asked when his father came back into the kitchen.

"It's the result of ingesting too much sugar. Your body crashes. Don't worry, she should be fine once she wakes up and eats a normal meal."

What Jake really wanted to know was where they had taken his real mother. This was an illusion of some kind. Perhaps it was goblin magic, he thought, the same kind used on his father so he couldn't see the goblin baseball players. He wished he could talk to his father about all of this.

"Dad, did you ever see things when you were young?" he asked instead.

"What kinds of things?"

"I don't know. Things no one else could see?"

His father looked at him for a long moment. After careful consideration of the question, he said, "I suppose all kids do, to some degree. I probably had an imagination a lot like yours, if that's what you're getting at."

If his father knew anything, Jake thought, he was good at concealing it.

Bottom of the 3ʳᵈ

He found an area near the long driveway leading to the folk house and began to dig, though his heart was not in it. It was one of the last few pieces of unbroken ground in Pine Barrows. In the all-out attempt to gain possession of the Sacred Amulet, the noble forest realm had been ransacked and defiled. Over time, the wounds would heal, but the land would be forever scarred.

After going down a full cubit and finding nothing in the hole, Lorcan moved on to dig in another spot and caught sight of a maple tree from which a circle of rubber was hanging by a length of hemp rope. He had watched the boy earlier as he tossed a baseball through the center and was amazed by the precision and velocity that the small human could hurl the ball. Lorcan loved baseball himself, as all goblins did, though he was never any good at it, especially pitching. He just couldn't throw. He would try, throwing as hard as it could, but the ball always went straight up in the air and land a few feet in front of him. His friends all laughed at him. So, he just stopped playing.

The adoration he had for the game was tempered only by his devotion to the folk house and his service to its human inhabitants. Because it had been abandoned for so long, there hasn't been a lot for him to do in recent years. He dug holes in search of the fabled Sacred Amulet to pass the time. He felt needed, though not because he had an allegiance to Buach or the evil goblin alliance seeking to possess its magic. Lorcan always thought the mysterious relic was not something that could be acquired, or even held in goblin hands. But he was told to dig, so that's what he did. However, now that the folk house was once again occupied, what he was being tasked with doing by the Order was in direct conflict with his sworn duty.

"Remain where you are, hogboon," Garbhan's voice boomed from the distance. Before Lorcan could see him, standing brush and tree limbs and small saplings were thrashed and splintered by the massive, spiked club that the creature wielded, cutting a swath through the forest as it approached.

Loran held his ground. The fachan was slow and easy to outrun, but because it was filled with such violence and hatred for all living things, it was not a creature to be trifled with or made angry.

It came into view, thundering toward Lorcan, hopping along on its thickly muscled leg. This was a true monster. It could evoke such terror that some humans were known to have died of fright at the mere glimpse of its ghastly features. Garbhan came to a stop with a loud thump directly in front of Lorcan. "What are you doing over here, hogboon?"

"This is where Ruadhan told me to dig."

"Never mind him," Garbhan snarled. His nose, with its single nostril, wiggled back and forth. His sense of smell was keen, which he used to try to get a whiff of Ruadhan's presence. He glanced around in all directions, knowing the pooka could take any form. There was no sign of him. Garbhan did not trust the shapeshifter, who clearly wanted to take his place in the hierarchy of the Order. The creature had overstepped many goblins already to get to his current position at number-three, and Ruadhan would not stop until he became Underlord. Garbhan would not allow that to happen.

"I've come with instructions for you, hogboon. Our Overlord has a task for you."

"He's not my Overlord," Lorcan grumbled.

"Your father was an elf, a Huldufolk. He might be able to make himself invisible, but you cannot. If you did not want to serve Buach, you should have left with the others when you had the chance, just crawled away on your belly with the very young and the very old who were not willing or able to serve."

"My service is to the folk house."

"The Order is only interested in what might be inside the folk house, which you will thoroughly explore in search of the Sacred Amulet." Garbhan elevated his club. "Lest you want another taste of my club. What Buach will do to you if you fail, will be far worse."

"I know, Peg Leg Jack," Lorcan said, knowing that addressing him by this name would raise the fachan's ire.

"No one calls me that." Garbhan's fist clenched around the handle of his club. "I would grind your bones to dust right now if Buach didn't have a task for you to perform."

"When Ruadhan outranks you, will you allow *him* to call you Peg Leg Jack, as you do Buach?"

"You are a troublemaker, hogboon. I will keep an eye on you."

"You should use that one eye to watch Ruadhan, who seeks to take your position."

A low growl resonated deep in Garbhan's throat. "I am not worried about him. I have the loyalty of Flann, the formidable red cap, on my side. He will do my bidding if I pay him his blood dues, which he knows I can deliver for him." As his voice rose in anger, so too did his arm before he swiftly brought the club down with such fearsome power that the ground shook underfoot.

Lorcan did not flinch. He had gotten under Garbhan's skin. The fachan, however, did not want to displease the Overlord, so Lorcan knew he would not be mortally harmed. At least not until Buach no longer had use for him. His unrestrained belligerence was his protection. It could not be assumed that he was working against the Order simply for expressing his discontent. In fact, Buach and his subjects, particularly Garbhan, enjoyed having someone to push around. All the other goblins who did not want to be a part of the Order, with the only exception being the goblins of the Resistance, had fled Pine Barrows. The only reason Lorcan stayed was because he did not want to abandon the folk house which he and his family had served for so many years. Now there was a new family living there, and he felt duty-bound to serve them.

There was, indeed, a price Lorcan had to pay for this loyalty, and the Order was more than willing to take advantage of it. Whatever importance the boy and his parents had to the warring factions, Lorcan was caught in the middle.

"I cannot tear up the floors and walls of the folk house," Lorcan told Garbhan. "Even if I wanted, I am incapable of causing damage to it."

"The Sacred Amulet will not be buried in the folk house," Garbhan explained. "It will be somewhere in plain view. It may be disguised as an everyday item, an object that you would never suspect contains such immense power."

"How will I know when I see it?"

"You will know," Garbhan assured him.

"Have you ever seen it?"

"Everyone who gazes upon the Sacred Amulet will see it differently."

It did not make much sense to the simple hogboon. "Will it be small enough for me to lift and transport?"

"You do not have sufficient magic to remove it yourself. A powerful incantation is required to displace the Sacred Amulet from its holding place and secure it for Buach to possess. Once you have located it, you must stand before it, or over it, and with your eyes closed and your heels touching, recite the magic words three times in succession, slowly increasing the volume of your voice and tonal range, and only opening your eyes during the third verse."

"So, let me understand this; not only do you want me to find some magical object which happens to look ordinary, but then you want me to put on some kind of floor show and sing a song to it. Do I have that right?"

"It is the only reason you are still alive, hogboon. I cannot stress enough how important this is. The folk house is the only place that hasn't been thoroughly searched. The Sacred Amulet must be inside somewhere."

"It looks like I've become pretty important around here."

"Do not overestimate your status, hogboon. When you become more trouble than you're worth, you will become immediately dispensable. And I will be more than happy to do the dispensing myself. The little power that the folk house affords you will not save you if you betray the Order. Buach will have no trouble leveling the folk house flat. The remains will be consumed by the natural world and become part of the forest again."

The infliction of physical harm by the fachan could only go skin deep, but the destruction of the folk house would be permanent. The area had been clear cut in the year 1636 and a three-story, timber-framed home, supported by massive tree trunks acting as support pillars, had been erected on the very spot where the folk house now stands. This was an historic place. It was where the game of baseball was actually invented and played for the first time by humans and goblins alike. Lorcan could not allow it to be destroyed.

"What's it going to be, hogboon?" Garbhan's fingers tightened around the handle of his club.

Lorcan didn't know what he would do if he was even able to recognize the Sacred Amulet. He couldn't allow himself to think about what would happen if he failed, but it was worse to think about what would happen to Pine Barrows if he succeeded. The Sacred Amulet was a neutralizing force, existing only to ensure a balance of power, a protection against dominance by any goblin faction. Everything would be destroyed if the Sacred Amulet fell into Buach's hands.

"I'm afraid I don't have much of a choice," Lorcan said.

"Very smart, hogboon." He leered triumphantly. "Now you're thinking clearly. I suggest you get started right away if you want this folk house to continue standing."

Garbhan made Lorcan memorize the incantation, repeating it until he knew it by heart. When the fachan stalked off, he issued a warning to Lorcan, who was too distracted with his own thoughts to hear exactly what threat had been directed against him. He did not feel good about what he had been asked to do.

As he wandered toward the clearing in the distance, the folk house came into view. He had seen the evolution of this homestead, beginning not long after Henry Tisdale arrived on the continent from England aboard the Mayflower and made his way to this remote region, which would become known as Pine Barrows. Tisdale, however, was not a Pilgrim, but part of another group that was quite different, known as Merchant Adventurers, or "Strangers" as the Pilgrims referred to them. These Strangers did not finance the trip themselves, but instead they enlisted the help of people in London who were interested in settling the new world strictly as a financial investment. Henry Tisdale came to the New World as a servant/apprentice to one of the Adventurers. On an expedition north-west into the Adirondacks with a group of Adventurers, Tisdale's wife suddenly died. While the other Adventurers continued, this was where Tisdale's voyage ended. Together with his five sons, a tract of land was cleared, and a three-story homestead was constructed. Lorcan's father began serving the Tisdale clan at that time.

Two hundred years later, the origins of baseball began on these very grounds. Rounders, which has some similarities to baseball, was already being played in Ireland and England at the time. The descendants of Henry Tisdale's family played Rounders in their own way. They used a Rowan tree branch for a bat and a rolled-up cloth for a ball, and imposed rules similar to what is seen in modern baseball today. Here in the Adirondacks, this new version of the game evolved and became increasing popular, not only with humans, but goblins as well. By the time Lorcan took over for his father, baseball was well established in all parts of the country.

Lorcan stopped beside Jake's maple tree. There was a baseball lying on the ground under the hanging tire. He had watched the boy throwing earlier and it looked like fun. Lorcan wanted to try it. It had been a long time since he threw a baseball. He picked up the ball and positioned himself a short distance away from the tire. Raising his arm, he cocked his hand behind his head and pushed his arm forward. The ball went = up into the air and came back down, striking his big toe.

"Ouch," he yelped. He reached down and grasped his foot in both hands. As he hopped in place on the other foot, he raised his throbbing toe to his mouth, suckling it. When he lowered his leg, his shoulders slumped and he drew out a long breath, remembering why he didn't play baseball.

At least no on saw him, he thought. No one to laugh at him.

If he were as good as the human boy, everything would be different. He wondered if the boy would teach him how to throw. He didn't think so, not after he'd taken the human woman and replaced her with a fetch. But he had a chance to make things right. There was still time.

Top of the 4th

Jake couldn't sleep. Lying in bed, he stared up at the ceiling thinking not only about where his mother might be and how to get her back, but about what Skip Blackburn told him about having goblin blood and how he was brought to Pine Barrows to help defeat a bunch of evil goblins. It was hard to believe. Among other things, it meant that Skip really didn't want his father to pitch for his team, and that made Jake feel bad. It wasn't fair. His father had worked really hard to get his arm back into condition to pitch again. For a long time, Jake didn't think his father would ever play baseball again, so he was very excited when his father got an offer to pitch, even from an independent league team.

Two seasons before, his father was having a spectacular first half with the AAA Storm Chasers. Midway through the season, he had a record of 9-1 with 1.51 ERA and a .89 WHIP, when suddenly it all went up in smoke. He was tossing a one-hit shutout entering the eighth inning when he released a first-pitch fastball to the leadoff hitter and felt a sharp pain in his right shoulder. His father told him later that he heard a dull popping sound and it felt like two knives were being jammed into his shoulder at the same time.

The news that his doctors gave him several days later was not good. Not only did the injury put an end to his season, by all accounts it was the end of his career. His father had sustained what is called a SLAP tear, a serious injury to a part of the shoulder joint called the labrum. It's the worst injury that a pitcher could have. Two operations and a year of rehab later, he was considered damaged goods and un-signable. But his father trained hard, and six months later he was poised for a comeback bid. After seven seasons, working his way up through the Minor Leagues, he wanted to give it one last bid at making it to the Majors before going into a family business, an asphalt paving company run by his two brothers in Queens.

"This is a real long shot," were the first words that came out of his father's mouth the day he made the announcement to his family about the offer by the Pine Barrows Mound Men. "I don't want either of you to get overexcited, but I recently got an offer from a team that wants me to pitch for them."

He barely finished the sentence before Jake jumped up, screaming with excitement.

"Hold on there, sport. I haven't agreed to anything yet. I told them I have to talk it over with my family first. This is a decision we all have to make. It affects all of us, and there are a couple factors to consider. The Pine Barrows Mound Men have no affiliation to the Major Leagues. This would be a situation where if I pitch well, then maybe I'll get noticed and I can get an opportunity to try-out for a big league team. But that's a big maybe. They also play in a very remote, isolated community in the Adirondack Mountains in upstate New York. I don't have to tell either of you what life on the road is like for minor league ballplayers and their families. It will be even worse with an independent club. They want me to be prepared for their short summer season, which starts next week, so if we do decide to go, we'll have to be packed and ready to hit the road right away."

Jake could barely contain his exhilaration when his father told them that his new manager had a place for them to stay, an old farmhouse not far from the field. His father did not say anything about his manager being a goblin who was in a civil war with evil goblins.

"I'm through talking," he said in conclusion. "Now I want to hear from you both."

His mother, who had always supported his father's baseball career, was smiling from ear to ear. Just picking up and moving to upstate New York was not something she would have given a second thought about if it meant the fulfillment of his father's dream of playing in the Majors. The two of them had been together since they were in high school. They were both attending Virginia Tech when they decided to get married in their junior year, exchanging vows in a ceremony while standing on the pitcher's mound of the school's baseball field.

Jake was born before they graduated. His father was drafted in the fifth round and signed with the Cleveland Indians. He began his pro career in rookie ball in Arizona and the three of them traveled together as a family no matter what far flung baseball outpost his father found himself in as he moved up through the different levels of the Minor Leagues with several different franchises. Over the years, they had lived in parts of twelve different states, staying for as little as a few weeks but never more than six months. Pine Barrows didn't sound that bad.

"You've been working so hard, honey," his mother began. "You deserve this chance. We're all in this together. I believe you can do it. I know Jake believes in you. And your new manager believes it. How about you?"

His father peered at them both. "Looks like it's unanimous," he said, a smile erupting across his face. "We're going to Pine Barrows."

They began jumping up and down and on top of one another, collapsing to the floor in a pig pile.

Jake was lost in this memory when he heard a scratching sound coming from the stairway.

It worked, he thought.

Before going to bed that night, Jake got to thinking about what Skip had said about being contacted by a goblin in the Resistance. He didn't want to wait, so he thought he could entice one to come to him. He remembered reading how goblins sometimes did chores in homes for people who left out sweets or sugary treats for them, so on his way to bed earlier, he left a slice of wild huckleberry pie in a bowl on the landing. His father bought the pie at the same roadside farm-stand along with the eggs.

Jake was excited and a little scared as he got out of bed, realizing that he had invited one of the creatures into the house. It was nearly three in the morning as he snuck out of his room to see what he could find. The hallway was dark, but he did not want to wake his parents, so he left the lights off. When he reached the top of the stairs, he peered down but could not see anything. He descended slowly. When he reached the bottom, he saw the dish on the landing. The pie was still in it and it had not been touched. Disappointment, together with a corresponding sense of relieve, overwhelmed him.

Then he caught a glimpse of movement out of the corner of his eye. He turned quickly in the direction of the kitchen, but whatever was there dashed off silently into deeper shadows.

"I see you," Jake said. He struggled to keep his voice from quivering. "Might as well come out." A moment later, to his utter surprise, a small creature emerged from the kitchen. Its stature and unique features were instantly familiar to Jake. "Hey, I saw you in the road yesterday."

The tiny man with narrow arms, bulging belly, and Pinocchio-like nose was the same one he had seen digging a hole in the road when his family first drove into Pine Barrows.

The goblin walked right up to him and stopped, all the while chomping feverishly on a piece of gum and blowing tiny bumbles. "I'm Lorcan."

"I'm Jake."

"Hi, Jake. Nice to meet you. Thank you for the libation. Some goblins take offense to such kindness, but not me."

"Libation?"

"The wild huckleberry pie you left on the stairs. It's my favorite."

Jake's brow wrinkled. He glanced around at the hunk of pie at the bottom of the staircase. "It doesn't look like you even touched it."

"We only consume the essence of human food."

"You can't get very full that way."

Lorcan snorted in amusement. "We have plenty of food, don't you worry. Goblins love to eat." He laid his hands atop his protruding belly, which jiggled as he laughed. "You just need to be careful which goblins you invite inside. Some are most unwelcome, indeed."

"Are you with Skip and the Resistance?" Jake asked.

Lorcan shook his head.

Jake started. "You are with Buach and the Order?"

"No."

"Who are you with then?"

"I'm not with anybody," Lorcan avowed. "I'm with the house. I have been doing chores here for many years, even when the folk house sat empty for so long before your family arrived. My father served the household before me."

"Well. I'm glad you are here, Lorcan. Maybe you can help me find out what happened to my mother."

The pot-bellied goblin dropped his head, staring down at his oversized bare feet. "I knew I shouldn't have done it," he sighed. "They used me."

"Who?"

"Buach and the others."

"So, you *are* with Buach." Jake charged.

Lorcan looked up. "No. They just made me do something I shouldn't have done."

"What did they make you do?"

The goblin hesitated, averting his eyes. "They made me take your mom."

"*You* took my mom? Where is she?"

Lorcan glanced all around as if to make sure no one else was there. "I don't know. I gave her to Ruadhan."

"Ruadhan? Who's that?"

"A shapeshifter. He most often appears as a black horse. He's part of the Order. He gave her to Buach." Lorcan hung his head in despair. "I'm sorry. I knew I shouldn't have done it, even if they threatened to destroy the folk house."

"Wait." Jake half-turned and pointed up the stairs. "Who's that upstairs if it's not my mother?"

"It's a fetch."

"What's that?"

"It's goblin magic. An enchanted object made to look like your mother. But the magic will soon wear off, and as it does, it will appear that your mother is unwell. She will get sicker." Lorcan hesitated a moment. "And then die," he said softly, as if to ease the impact of the reality.

"What about my real mother?"

"Well, since she was taken into the goblin world, she will remain there forever if she does not return to the human world before the magic animating the fetch wears off."

Jake gasped. He blinked rapidly to dry the tears collecting in the corner of his eyes. "How long before the magic wears off?"

"In human time, not long. A day or two. Not much more."

Jake took a deep breath. "We have to get my mother back. I need to find Buach. You must help me."

Lorcan's eyes bulged with terror. "You don't want to do that. It would be too dangerous. Buach is evil."

"I don't care. He has my mother. How can I find him?"

"His fortress is secret. No one knows where it is. Powerful magic conceals the entrance."

"You must have some way to reach him, Lorcan. Please."

"He has underlings who do his bidding, usually Garbhan, a most foul goblin. He boasts of an alliance with Flann, a bloodthirsty goblin that he sways with the promise of fresh blood from human victims. You want to keep your distance from both of them. But it was Garbhan who gave me a task to perform here tonight. Though, I admit I came for another reason all my own."

"What were you sent here to do?"

"The Order seeks the Sacred Amulet, a powerful talisman. Buach is digging up all of Pine Barrows to find it. That's what you saw me doing in the road. But it hasn't been located yet, and they think it may be somewhere inside this house. Because I have unfettered access here, they want me to find it for them. I would have you know that should Buach come to possess the Sacred Amulet, the Order will defeat the Resistance, and Buach would rule over Pine Barrows for a thousand years."

"I see." Jake believed the goblin to be sincere. "You do not want the Order to possess the Sacred Amulet, do you?"

"No. My service is to this house, not the Order, and not Buach."

Jake noticed an irregular bruise on the Goblin's cheek. "They will harm you if you do not bring them the Sacred Amulet?"

Lorcan touched his cheek and nodded in silence.

"Seems like we both have a lot to lose," Jake said. He smiled at Lorcan, who smiled back at him. "You said you had another reason for being here. What is that?"

Lorcan lowered his head slightly, his large cobalt eyes gazing tentatively at the boy. "I was sort of hoping, well, that you would teach me how to throw a baseball."

"You want *me* to teach you?"

"Yes. I've seen you throw. And you're really good."

"You think so?"

"Certainly. The other day I saw you throw all those baseballs right through the middle of the circular target hanging from the old maple tree. You hardly missed any. After what I've done, I don't suppose you would consider teaching me?"

Jake laughed. "I'd be happy to teach you, Lorcan. I just wouldn't want you to get in any trouble with Buach. He wants to ban goblins from playing in Pine Barrows."

"That's all right. He would only laugh, like everyone else. I'm not very good. Actually, I'm terrible."

"Let's see what we can do about that then. But first, I have to figure out how to get my mom back before it's too late."

"I believe you can stop Buach," Lorcan said. "I haven't been around very many humans, but there is something special about you."

That made Jake smile. He said goodbye to Lorcan, who waved as he walked away, disappearing into the shadows of the kitchen. When the goblin was gone, Jake wondered what he could possibly do to preserve the folk house for Lorcan, save Pine Barrows from Buach, and most of all get his mother back from the goblin world. Maybe the Resistance could help, he thought. Skip would know what to do.

With everything that was on his mind, he didn't think he would be able to fall asleep, but he was so exhausted he went out the instant his head touched the pillow.

Bottom of the 4th

They danced around in front of the low wooden stage like men possessed, leaping and gamboling in rhythm to the folk music. Their movements were strange and fascinating at the same time. They formed a large circle, kicking up their feet and flailing their arms in a kind of mad waltz. These revelers and the members of the four-piece string band playing for them were all goblins.

The kerosene lamps and candles that illuminated the dance floor cast deep shadows on the interior of the dance hall as well as on the features of everyone inside. Misshapen heads, pointy noses and elongated ears were exaggerated. All were members of the Resistance, the Mound Men players and their families. The wives and girlfriends wore long gowns that fluttered up as the men whipped them around, exposing legs resembling those of elk, deer, and other forest-dwelling animals. One poor goblin girl had the legs and hindquarters of a cow. The ones who wore open toe shoes, or were barefooted, revealed feet that ended in cloven hooves.

Prank stood out in the group even though he was not among the biggest or more exotic of goblins. His large eyes glowed brightly, and a long, downward-turned nose almost touched his chin. He was high-spirited, to put it mildly.

Every major muscle movement and minor flinch he made was quick and sure, and his exaggerated motions stirred up his full head of long, shaggy brown hair.

He spoke with great exuberance, oftentimes when he shouldn't, including when he had food in mouth. In that regard, however, he was no different than the other goblins in attendance. To a human, it was unfathomable how much goblins could eat. Prank shoveled food into his mouth continuously all night long. Spare bear ribs, fried frog appetizers, salamander soup, fresh greens, potatoes, vegetables, and all kinds of desserts. He devoured an entire basket of bread by himself and countless glasses of wine to wash it all down. Nothing seemed to quench his appetite. And he wasn't the only one who ate like he had two stomachs. The other players gorged themselves as well, and still had room to spare. They raced through dinner at record speed, talking and telling jokes the whole time. Prank was making everyone laugh with his imitations of Skip and many of the Mound Men players, changing his speech patterns and gesticulations to mimic them.

When a fiddler and a banjo player burst out with a rousing rendition of Flop-Eared Mule, everyone in the room jumped up at once, led by Prank. The dance floor filled instantly with a troupe of goblins, some with drinks and food in their hands. Their bodies became a blur as they moved and spun about in a dizzying manner.

Skip sat alone at a table beside his wife. He was tapping his feet to the beat when his wife rose and asked him to join her on the dance floor. To his dismay and confusion, he found that he was unable to get out of his chair. When he failed after a more vigorous attempt, Prank's boisterous laughter could not be drowned out by the music, and that's when Skip realized he was literally glued to his chair. His back, legs, butt, even his arms were locked in place and he was unable to move. Turning his head toward the dance floor, Skip smiled good-naturedly at Prank, who acknowledged responsibility for his manager's dilemma by holding up a jar of sap.

"Good one, you got me," Skip said, silently chastising himself for not checking the unoccupied chair beside Prank before he sat down. The natural glue was deluded and wasn't permanent, but the bond was strong enough to temporarily immobilize him.

He resolved to be a good sport about it and just wait it out when suddenly the walls, floor and ceiling began to flicker as the magic accommodating their gathering began to wane. At first, Skip thought it might be Prank's doing, but he knew there could only be one thing interfering with the spell.

As the spell wore off, the dance hall dissolved and the forest reappeared. The intervening darkness was deeper and more pervasive than the moonless night sky. As the goblins scattered, taking up positions in protected safe zones, as was protocol in such emergencies, Skip struggled to free himself. With limited mobility, he could not use magic to counteract the effect of the glue that incapacitated him. In conjunction with a spoken incantation, his arms were required to initiate any magic spell.

Prank, who felt responsible for his manager's predicament, scrambled to reach him. He was only a few feet away from Skip, but powerful magic prevented him from getting any closer. A wall of black nothingness that he could not penetrate separated him from Skip.

"Curse you, Buach," Skip spat. His redoubled efforts to disengage himself from the chair were futile.

Preceded by his miniature army of goblin misfits mounted on the backs of chickens, Buach made his appearance. As he drew nearer, his posse surrounded the manager of the Mound Men, who had stopped thrashing. There was no escape. The Overlord drew right up to him, his face so close that Skip could feel the heat from Buach's eyes singe his cheeks.

"Blackburn," Buach hissed. "It's been a long time."

"Excuse me for not getting up."

Buach laughed. "I see you're still wasting your magic, when you have so little of it, on such foolish merriment." He clicked his forked tongue, which made a sharp sound, like a cracking whip.

"Life is a gift to be enjoyed."

"Silly folk logic."

"This *foolish merriment*, as you call it, is the reason they resist you and your powerplay to destroy all that they love."

Buach laughed again. "Your feeble forces are no match for the Order. You have no means to defend yourself against our might."

"A good cause finds weapons to protect it."

"Just more folk logic. Cling to that if it makes you feel better, Blackburn. But know this: I will destroy you and the other members of the Resistance one by one. You keep moving your games to different places in Pine Barrows, thinking I will not find you, but I have proven that I can always get to you. Your power is weak and getting weaker all the time. There are less goblins playing baseball, and the magic it produces continues to diminish. You will not be able to sustain your resistance movement much longer. It is just a matter of time."

"You do not have near the power you presume to possess," Skip said evenly.

"Said the goblin who couldn't even get up out of his chair."

"If you have sufficient power to overtake the entire Resistance, why have you not done so already? You barely have enough to overtake me, and in the condition that I'm in right now, it doesn't take much." Skip wiggled his arms in vain to demonstrate his immobility.

"You're right about one thing, Blackburn. I could destroy you right now. But I intend to vanquish the entire Resistance movement."

"Then you are too late." Skip smiled knowingly. "So, you may as well take me and be happy with that, for it is *your* demise that is imminent."

Skip's smug grin infuriated Buach. "Your folk logic is wearing thin with me. I do not fear you."

"It is not me you should fear."

"Who then?"

Skip paused for dramatic effect. "The human boy who resides in the folk house."

The laughter that erupted from the Overlord's foul maw was genuine and sustained, and it doubled him over before he was able to speak again. "You expect me to be fearful of a human boy?"

"*This* human boy, yes," Skip said definitively. He may have overplayed the otherkin's ability and his ultimate influence on the outcome of the goblin war between the Order and the Resistance, but he had to play that card to buy some time and give the boy a chance. It was the only hope.

Buach grinned. "Okay, I'll bite. What's so special about him?"

"He's an otherkin," Skip said boldly.

"You lie."

"Both his parents possess goblin blood. His powers are great. Untapped, but certainly more than you possess. And when he finds the Sacred Amulet, he will destroy you and restore Pine Barrows to its former glory."

"By your own folk logic, if what *you* say is true, the boy doesn't know of his powers, or where the Sacred Amulet is hidden, otherwise he would have already destroyed the Order."

"Are you willing to take that chance?" Skip looked relaxed seated in the chair, as if he weren't fastened to the wood by pitch glue. "Don't forget, Buach, I know why you are the way you are; so angry, hateful and jealous."

"You think you can know the mind of Buach? You know nothing."

"It was a long time ago, but I remember. I may be the only who remembers. When you were young. I was coach of a junior baseball team you tried out for."

"ENOUGH!"

The flames in Buach's eyes flared bright red. The heat they discharged raised the temperature in the air directly around Skip.

"Assuming that you are telling the truth," the Overlord raged, "you may have bought yourself a little extra time, but the presence of this otherkin will not save you. Rest-assured, I will deal with the boy. In the meantime, tell the others in the Resistance that there is no escape. They cannot win. I will give you until the next full moon to surrender. That's two days. If you give up, I will not destroy any of you. Your goblins will be enslaved, becoming vassals in the Order, but they will live. Tell them. You can be the instrument of their demise or the mode of their salvation. It's up to you."

Buach suddenly turned and left, trailed by his minions. As the Overlord disappeared, his magic dissipated, and Prank and the other goblins of the Resistance were able to reach the manager.

"Skip, are you okay?" Prank asked. "I'm sorry about this."

"No harm done. I'm fine." Skip grinned knowingly. "We have a real chance now," he said. "A chance we didn't have before the otherkin arrived."

Top of the 5th

Jake woke with a start to bright sunlight streaming in through the east-facing window. Realizing he had overslept, in a panic he jumped out of bed without looking and slipped on a scattering of books and binders strewn across the floor. He lost his balance and tumbled backwards. His fall was broken by the now-empty boxes that had previously contained the baseball periodicals and notebooks he was sitting amidst.

He got to his feet and surveyed the chaos around the room, wondering what happened. He knew the boxes and their contents had been stored and stacked in an orderly fashion along the walls of his bedroom when he went to sleep the night before. There were empty chewing gum wrappers everywhere and it occurred to him that it had to be Lorcan.

But why? Was he looking for the Sacred Amulet? Had the goblin lied when he said he wasn't working for Buach?

This thought troubled him as he quickly dressed, grabbed his baseball cap and glove from the bedpost, and headed out the door. He had to talk to Skip, tell him about Lorcan and come up with a plan to save his mother. He was looking back at the mess in his room when he stepped into the hallway and bumped into his dad.

"Whoa! What's the hurry, sport?"

"Sorry, Dad. I overslept."

"I know. I looked in on your earlier and saw your books all over the place, so I let you sleep. I figured you were up late looking at them because you couldn't sleep, worrying about your mother."

"Yeah. How's she doing?"

"I don't know what's wrong with her. She doesn't have a fever and she's not in any pain. She's just tired and weak, which is really strange because of the way she has been eating. She had a snack of cookies and cream cheese in the middle of the night, and this morning I made her pancakes and sausage. There's some left in the refrigerator for you, but you better get to them before your mother does."

The magic was starting to wear off, Jake thought. There wasn't much time. He had to find out where Buach was keeping her before it was too late.

"She's been acting really peculiar, too," his father said. "One minute she's laughing like a giddy schoolgirl and the next minute she's crying. The only thing we can do is go back to the city to see a doctor. I'm going to practice in a little while. I'll tell Skip."

"You mean leave Pine Barrows?" Jake asked. A chill ran through his veins. If they left now, the magic animating the fetch would wear off while they were gone and his real mother would remain in the goblin world forever. "What about the Mound Men? This is your last chance."

His father leaned over and braced his son's head gently between the palms of his big hands. "I know you had your heart set on seeing me get a shot at playing in the Bigs. It's disappointing for me, too, but your mom's health is more important."

"Yeah," Jake said. A tear slipped out of the corner of one eye and ran down his cheek.

"Your mother's going to be just fine. I promise."

Jake believed him.

"And if my playing again is meant to be, I'll get another chance."

A car horn sounded outside.

"They're here for me," his father said. "You gonna be okay for a little while? Or I could just stay home. Let me run down and tell the driver."

"No, that's okay, Dad. I'll be all right. Really."

"Ok. I'll be back in a few hours. Your mother just fell asleep. Let her rest. She may sleep the whole afternoon. In the meantime, you can start putting your things together." He paused. "I'm sorry, sport," he said, drying Jake's cheek with the back of his hand. He turned and headed down the stairs. A moment later the front door opened and closed.

Jake walked to the other end of the hallway and peered out the window overlooking the driveway, where a van was parked in front of the house. The goblin sitting in the driver's seat looked directly up at him and waved. Jake instinctively waved back. He watched his father get into the vehicle with his bag and drive away.

Jake was still confident he could get to the field before his father. The fort was his own private portal to the goblin world.

On his way to the stairs, he stopped in front of his mother's bedroom and put his ear close to the door. There was no sound coming from inside. Reaching up, he grasped the doorknob and gently turned it. The latch clicked softly, and he pushed the door inward just enough to see inside. In the bed, resting on the pillow, was a tree branch. He carefully pulled the door closed and hurried downstairs.

After choking down a couple of cold pancakes from the refrigerator, he inhaled a juice box on his way out the door and headed toward the fort. The sky was now overcast and grim. Dark clouds swirled ominously, and blustery winds buffeted him from all directions, almost knocking him off his feet. Something about this weather did not seem natural to Jake, making him wonder if it was something generated by Buach.

The intensity of the wind increased, most of it blasting straight out of the woods at him. It wasn't like being in a hurricane or tornado, or at least what Jake imagined those things would be like. It was more like being in front of a jet engine. The roar was deafening. It slowed him to a near halt, but he fought it, lowering his shoulders and pumping his legs as hard as he could. He quickly grew tired, and his forward progress stopped. The force of the wind stood him up and flipped him backward. He tumbled and rolled several times before coming to a stop. Lying on his stomach, he dug his fingers into the soil and turned his face to one side to protect his eyes from flying dirt and debris.

That low to the ground, the strength of the wind was weakest, and he found that he could crawl forward at a slow but steady pace. Leaves and branches swept past at great speeds. The mightiest trees groaned and creaked, while smaller and weaker ones were splintered by the powerful gusts. Suddenly, something sharp nicked the top of his upturned left ear. The air rushing over the minor laceration at such speed stung considerably, but he kept moving. He looked up when he crossed the tree line, trying to blindly locate the fort in the swirling darkness and under the canopy of violently swaying trees.

He did not see the fort until it was right in front of him. The opening was blocked by a large broken tree branch. All its leaves had been stripped bare. Placing both hands on the splintered end, he lifted it vertically. When it was nearly upright, the wind caught it and blew it away like a twig.

Jake did not waste any time crawling inside the fort. Exhausted, he collapsed while the fury of the storm continued outside. He was safe, at least for the moment. From the battering that the structure was taking, he wasn't sure it would hold up much longer. The biggest trees all around were ripped from the ground by their roots, thick trunks snapped in half like pretzel rods. Somehow, the wooden frame around him held fast, the tree sap working better than concrete, the walls and roof bending and flexing, but not breaking.

Bottom of the 5th

All at once the storm just stopped, and that's how long it took Jake to realize that he had been transported into the goblin world. He lifted his head, his ear stinging and wet with drying blood. He got to his feet and stood upright in the tunnel beneath the baseball field. He made his way to the dugout, but as soon as he emerged, he knew something was wrong. The field was dark and empty. It was full night and moonless. The stars in the sky looked cold and dead, like distant points of ice rather than fire. As he wandered out to the mound, he thought he was either way too early or very late.

Then, there was movement from the trees behind the left field boundary. He watched as the figure pushed its way through the shrubs and moved toward him.

A smile broke out on his face. "Sk..." he began, stopping the instant he realized it was not the manager of the Mound Men. His smile dissolved.

He couldn't tell who or what it was at first, but it was menacing. It made a heavy clattering sound with each step, and it was carrying some kind of handheld weapon. Jake's breath caught in his throat when he realized there was nowhere to hide. It was so dark that it was only when the creature stopped and was standing right in front of him that he got his first good look at the intruder.

It was only about four feet in height, but just as wide. Long, unkempt hair hung down in front of its bloodshot eyes. Sharp, horned teeth protruded upward from the corners of its lower jaw. Its fingers tapered to jagged claws and it wore a long green coat and boots of iron. In its grasp was a long pikestaff that appeared to have seen a lot of action. Most prominent was the red stocking cap atop its head. It was dark red and wet.

"Beware the wicked red cap, he'd love to see you dead," a voice whispered. "He'll take all of your blood and wear it on his head."

Jake turned to face the whisperer, a dark-haired goblin with molten eyes.

"His name is Flann," the beast said. "He enjoys killing. Indeed, his very existence depends on it as his cap must remain coated with blood or *he* will die. Hence, he must frequently hunt and kill to keep his skullcap damp with fresh blood."

"Blood," Flann said, his voice deep and guttural. Jake froze in terror, unable to move as the monster raised its left arm and pressed the spiked tip of a finger to the cut on Jake's ear. A drop of blood was transferred onto the red cap's lethal digit, which it brought to its lips. "Blood," it said again as it licked the finger clean.

Jake's eyes were wide with terror, and he flinched, momentarily considering fleeing.

"Running is no use. Don't let Flann's awkward appearance deceive you. Red caps are supernaturally fast."

"You're Buach." Jake stated, daring to turn his back on the murderous creature to face the goblin Overlord. "Where is my mom? Take me to her right now!"

"I can do that," Buach said, nodding. "But you must do something for me."

"Anything."

A crooked smile played at the corners of Buach's mouth. "All you have to do is convince Skip Blackburn to give up. When the Resistance surrenders to me, she will be freed. Unharmed. If you cannot do that, well, let's just say that Flann's cap will be saturated with a fresh coat of blood."

Jake didn't think he had any other choice but to trust the beast. "You promise to let her go."

"You have my word."

The red cap's boots clanked as he took a half stride forward. Now no more than a couple inches separated Jake and the creature.

"I know what you are," Buach acknowledged. "As an otherkin, you have hidden power. More than you know. You can help the Resistance. Or you can save your mother. You can't do both. What's it going to be? She doesn't have a lot of time."

"Let me see her," he demanded. "I want to be sure she's all right first."

Buach shuttered his glowing eyes and inhaled deeply. With the fire sealed behind his eyelids, the field was engulfed in total darkness. The red cap dissolved from sight, as did everything else. The stars in the sky were extinguished and the background changed. Jake suddenly found himself inside of a massive candle-lit cavern honeycombed with a labyrinth of tunnels. Stalactites projected from the ceiling like dinosaur teeth and the walls shimmered with crystals of calcium carbonate that reflected the light from the candles.

This must be Buach's lair, Jake thought. But the beast was nowhere in sight. Directly in front of him was a sheer rock face with a large entryway at the bottom.

He approached the entrance with caution, pausing to remove a candle from the wall before going inside. While only able to see a couple of feet in front of him at a time, he found the ground floor to be a large, empty sanctuary. Locating a set of stone steps cut into the rock, he ascended to the floor above, where a series of small cells with iron bars lined both sides of a long hallway. He approached the nearest cell, but the candlelight did not stretch very far, making it appear empty. He detected soft whisperings, however. Many voices, all laden with fear, converged from all around. Then, out of the darkness at the back of the cell in front of him, a goblin appeared at the edge of the candlelight. He was small and frail, his gray face gaunt. Rigid bones protruded from his hairless naked torso. Large eyes with wide pupils inspected him.

"It's not Buach," the goblin announced to the others, his voice faint and coarse from not speaking for a lengthy period of time. "It's a human."

"I'm Jake. What's your name?"

"I am Diarmuid."

"Why have you been imprisoned?"

"Buach." The goblin's lower lip quivered at the mere mention of the name. "He told all the goblins of Pine Barrows who did not want to join the Order that we could travel to the nearest goblin kingdom to seek refuge. Instead, he imprisoned us."

The goblins in the other cells approached their bars tentatively. Jake held the candle out in front him, but there was no way to determine how many cells there were or how many goblins were being confined, but he could hear their movements, their clawed hands on the iron bars, which weakened them further, made them more submissive. He walked the length of the hallway. There were goblins in every cell, sometimes more than one. With eyes that had grown accustomed to absolute darkness, the prisoners strained to get a look at the visitor.

"Are you here to save us?" one of them asked.

Jake approached the cell which contained a large black horse. "Are you the shapeshifter, Ruadhan?"

The horse transformed into a large white owl. "I am," the bird replied.

"Lorcan told me that you are part of the Order. He said that you took my mother and gave her to Buach."

"That is a specious claim."

"What does that mean?"

"It means he is partially correct. I gave your mother to Buach, that is true, but I am with the Resistance."

"I don't understand."

"You might say that I was a double-agent. I infiltrated the Order and slowly gained Buach's trust, rising up in rank. Being in his inner circle, I was able to provide valuable information to Skip and help the Resistance. Buach recently discovered this tactic and imprisoned me."

"But why did you take my mother?" Jake's voice rose in exasperation.

"To get you to save her," Ruadhan said matter-of-factly. "Skip knew that it would rally you into action, so to speak. And in doing so, you would defeat Buach."

Jake paused a moment to process this information. "You mean all of this was *planned* by Skip? Having you infiltrate the Order so you could take my mother and give her to Buach? He used me. You all did."

"All of the goblins imprisoned here have made sacrifices." The owl's yellow eyes were partially closed and blood shot. They looked tired. "When our queen died and Buach seized power, we were doomed to live in constant fear, and some paid the ultimate price. Buach doesn't trust anyone, so when he found out I was a secret member of the Resistance, he blamed Garbhan, his Underlord, and had him killed by the red cap."

Flann's hat was dark red, Jake recalled, and it appeared wet.

"I expected that Buach would eventually discover who I was and would punish me severely. I am resigned to the same fate as Garbhan. It is for the greater good of all the goblins in Pine Barrows. And for baseball. My actions helped bring you here. Now it's up to you."

"But what can *I* do?"

"You are an otherkin. You have great power."

"Everyone keeps saying that. You think I can defeat Buach and save all of you, but I can't."

"The human boy is correct." Buach's imposing voice chased the goblins back into the dark recesses of their cells. "I've tried to tell them that there is no hope, but they don't listen to me. Maybe they will believe you." The Overlord manifested slowly out of the darkness. His eyes blazed but the dungeon somehow grew darker still. It was almost as if he was the darkness itself, absorbing every last ray of light.

"You promised to let me see my mother."

"Indeed, I did." He directed a taloned finger at the next cell, which had no bars at all.

Jake stepped inside and made his way to the back of the cell. There was stone bench covered with rags. On top, his mother lay reclined on her back. He placed the candle on the floor at his feet and bent down to look at her. Her eyes were closed.

"Mom? Can you hear me?" Grasping her around the shoulders, he shook her gently. She remained still, unmoving. "What's the matter with her?"

"She's sleeping." Buach's voice was mockingly comforting.

"She's dying," Jake snapped. "Release her from this spell right now."

"I'll do that as soon as you give me what I want."

Jake touched his mother lightly on the crown of her head, pulling back a few stray strands of hair from her face. "I'm going to save you," he whispered to her. Tears began to well in his eyes. He quickly wiped them away, not wanting to cry in front of Buach. "I love you, Mom." He picked up the candle and walked out of the cell, where Buach was waiting for him. "Why do you have all these goblins imprisoned?" he pointedly asked the Overlord.

Buach's eyes, which had tapered down to simmering embers, flared into a mini conflagration. "That is no concern of yours," he roared, his voice resounding like thunder.

Refusing to back down, Jake said, "They did not pose a threat to you. Why didn't you just let them leave Pine Barrows as you promised?"

"What I do with them is my business." The intensity of the fire in the beast's eyes diminished the flame from the candle, making the darkness almost absolute. "Do we have a deal or not?"

"Before I do what you want, you must let all of these goblins free."

Buach laughed, his thick, yellow teeth clacking, the sound reverberating around the chamber. "You do what I want *first*, and then I will free every last one of them."

Jake wavered. Buach had misled the goblins, telling them they could take refuge in another goblin kingdom, but instead he locked them in prison cells. Buach would surely lie to him just as easily as he had lied to his own kind.

"Well, otherkin? What's the hold up? Time is not a luxury you possess."

"Why should I trust you? My father says you can't trust anyone who doesn't like baseball."

"What does he know?"

"My dad is a great pitcher."

Buach scoffed. "I'm sure he is. *For a human.* He's no competition for a goblin team."

"I've seen him pitch against goblins. He blew them away."

"You mean the Mound Men?" Buach scoffed again, louder. "They're nothing. Your father wouldn't stand a chance against any nine goblins in the Order."

"He could beat *any* goblin team. Including yours."

"I don't play baseball anymore."

"That's because you know you'll lose."

Buach went completely rigid. It was as if he had turned to stone. Several moments before he moved again. Suddenly his jaw slackened and then he spoke. "Is that a challenge?"

Jake nodded without hesitation.

"I accept." Buach's black hair appeared to lighten several shades as he extended his hand.

When Jake grasped it, Buach laughed heartily and shoved him backward with tremendous force. In the same instant, a powerful gust of air sent him tumbling headlong down the hallway in utter darkness.

What have I done? Jake thought.

All the while, Buach's laughter echoed behind him.

Top of the 6th

Jake came to rest on his backside, looking up at the roof of the fort. He crawled out, unprepared for what he would see. The devastation was beyond belief. Every tree within a three-hundred-foot radius was in splinters. The tiny structure stood alone amid the destruction. He had to clamber over and under trunks of massive, downed trees. It took a while to traverse the short distance back to the yard at the back of the property.

He couldn't be sure what time it was, or what day for that matter. Time was different in the goblin world. Traveling through the portal didn't just take him to a different place, it took him to a different place in time. It was still daylight, so that was a good sign. And everything else looked exactly the same. The house and the property around it remained untouched. The windstorm's fury had been confined to a small area of the woods.

As he made his way around to the front of the farmhouse, he saw a strange car in the driveway. A wave of panic radiated throughout his body as he recalled a story that he read in fourth grade, *Rip Van Winkle*, about a man who got drunk with some ghosts and fell asleep for twenty years. When Rip Van Winkle woke up, everything was different and there was not a single person alive that he once knew. Jake pondered the possibility that it was twenty years later, and a new family was living there.

He walked up to the car, a green Subaru with New Hampshire tags and a vanity plate that read: COLECTR. The windows were down and no one was inside. Looking up at the farmhouse, he remembered that his Aunt Briget lived in New Hampshire. He had only met her once when he was about six and he had little recollection of her. His mother didn't speak much about Aunt Briget, but it was clear they didn't get along. He didn't know why she would be here now, unless his father had contacted her and told her about her sister not feeling well.

It was quiet inside the house. He proceeded upstairs, turning his ear to his mother's closed door before opening it a crack and peeking inside. The tree branch rested on the pillow, and his aunt was nowhere in sight.

The muffled sound of something crashing to the floor in the basement drew his attention. This was an area of the house he hadn't explored yet. On his way down to the stairs, he could see into the kitchen and the dim rectangle of light that was the open basement door.

As he got nearer, he heard objects being moved around.

"Auntie Briget," he called out.

There was no response, so he started down the concrete steps. The basement was damp and cool. It was a massive room cluttered with boxes, old furniture, and unknown objects covered with once-white sheets. Dust drifted down like dirty snow, coating everything in a gray film. At the far end of the basement, someone was sorting through the contents of a large box.

He was about to call his aunt again when he kicked a chunk of broken crockery that he hadn't noticed on the floor. It crumbled into smaller pieces as it skidded along the dirty concrete. Looking down, he saw a box laying on its side with broken plates and saucers spilling out. When he looked back up, his aunt was peering at him from behind an old piece of furniture. Her lips stretched like elastic bands as she smiled. "My, my," she began. "Who is this handsome young man?" Her voice was syrupy sweet.

"I'm Jake."

"No, you're not," she said as she walked up to him. "You can't be. Jake Lupo was no bigger than a garden gnome the last time I saw him. I'm your Aunt Briget. Let me get a look at you." She put her hands on his shoulders. "Why, you're almost as tall as I am. You must be what, fifteen, sixteen-years old?"

"Eleven-going-on-twelve."

She took a half step back, feigning shock. "I never would have guessed. You're going to be tall, like your dad. Do you play baseball, too?"

He shrugged. "We're here because my dad's trying out for independent team."

"I know. Your mom just told me all about it. That's really exciting."

"You talked to my mom?"

"We just had a nice conversation over lunch. I brought some fruits and vegetables at a roadside farm. She ate all of it and then nodded off. There was no one home, so while she was resting, I had a look around the house and wandered down here. This is an amazing house. There are pieces down here that are probably original furnishings, which means they were here when the house was first built."

Jake shifted his position as he surveyed the musty room and his foot raked over a small scattering of broken pottery.

"Be careful, honey," she warned. "Sorry about the mess. I'll get it cleaned up. Those plates are ceramic. They're old, but they're not worth anything." She guided him back toward the stairs. "Come on. Let's get out of the here. I have something for you."

When they got up to the kitchen, she closed the basement door and locked it. In the same motion, she reached for a large gold gift bag that was sitting on the countertop and handed it to Jake.

"What's this?" he asked.

"Look inside."

He reached in and pulled out a Native American bow and arrow. The wood was wrapped with buckskin, accented with fur, and finished with fringe and brass coned feathers. The two-foot long sinew quiver was wrapped with a bone tip.

"Whoa! Is it real?" Jake asked.

"It's a wall display. It's not for functional use. Your parents wouldn't take too kindly to you owning a dangerous weapon like that. But as replicas go, it's a perfect likeness of the real thing."

"It's really cool. Thanks, Auntie."

"You're welcome, dear." She flashed a triumphant smile. "Do you know what I do for a living?" she asked.

Jake shook his head.

"I'm an antiquarian."

"What's that?"

"It's a big ten-dollar word. It just means that I'm an antique collector. I look for old things that people don't want anymore. I buy some of them and fix them up, and then I find someone who is seeking just such an item and sell it to them. Some of the items are so rare and valuable that individuals will pay a great deal of money for them."

"Why would someone get rid of something that is so valuable?"

"That's a very good question," She told him. "The answer is that some folks may not have the same appreciation for a particular object that another person might have for it. Or it could be that the item is of no use to one person, but it could mean the world to someone else."

"Or maybe the person doesn't know that they have something of such value," Jake added.

She raised her eyebrows and nodded in agreement. "You're absolutely right. Sometimes people just don't know what they have."

"Is that why you came here? To look for antiques?"

"I wanted to surprise your mom and dad. And see my favorite nephew."

Jake had a suspicion that his aunt wasn't telling him everything. Maybe she knew about the goblins of Pine Barrows, but he dared not ask because that would reveal his own knowledge about them, which was something he couldn't even tell his father.

"Is there something else on your mind, dear?"

"Huh"

"You look like you want to ask me something?"

"I was just wondering if you were going to stay for a while."

She smiled, crinkling up her nose in playful manner. "I can stay as long as I am needed."

A short while later his father came home. He seemed pleased that Aunt Briget was there. They went right upstairs to see how his mother was doing. Jake didn't want to go, but his father compelled him to come along. This time, instead of a rowan tree branch, he saw a likeness of his mother. He lingered in the back of the room while the three of them talked. After just a couple minutes, his father announced that they would leave so his mother could get some more rest.

Jake didn't say much at dinner. After they finished eating, he got up to clean off the table, piling the dishes on the kitchen counter.

"Such a good boy," Aunt Briget said as she kissed him on the side of the forehead. "I'm going to turn in. It was a long drive up here."

"Goodnight, Aunt."

His father carried her suitcase up to the guest bedroom as he filled the kitchen sink with warm water. He had to scrub really hard to remove the dried meat pie from the plates. A short while later his father came back down and helped him by drying and putting away the dinnerware and utensils.

"I know it's difficult," his father began. "Your mom isn't acting like herself lately, but she's still your mother."

Jake looked at him and nodded in acknowledgement but didn't say anything, then turned his attention back to scouring the stubborn bits of meat from a fork.

"As far as your aunt goes," his father went on to say, "she and your mother may not exactly see things eye to eye, but it's good that they're reconnecting, especially now. After not speaking for so many years, maybe they can finally work things out."

"Why haven't they spoken for so long?"

"It's complicated, sport."

Jake stared silently back at his father, who after a long moment placed the cup he was drying on the counter, glanced out through that archway at the staircase to be sure it was empty, and then guided his son to the table. "Have a seat." His father sat across from him. "You're almost twelve, and I think you're old enough now to know some things." His voice was barely above a whisper. "The problem between your aunt and mother had to do with their mother's house. Your aunt had been living in the house with your grandmother, who you were too young to remember. When your grandmother got sick, she went into a nursing home where she could be better cared for. Your aunt bought the house so she could live there after Grandma died. Then, about six years ago, she sold the house. They haven't talked since then."

"How come?"

His father peeked out at the staircase again and then leaned in closer to Jake. "Apparently, when your grandfather died, he possessed a large collection of silver and gold coins. They were hidden under the floorboards and in the walls all around the house. I don't know exactly how much these coins were worth, but your aunt didn't share them with your mother. It wasn't for herself that your mother felt betrayed. She thought your aunt took something that belonged to you. Do you understand?"

"I think so," Jake responded. It made him think that Aunt Briget was more of a treasure hunter rather than an antique collector.

"It's best that they let bygones be bygones. Life's too short. And your aunt's arrival couldn't have come at a better time. It's really a blessing in disguise."

"What do you mean?"

"Well, I found out today that we're going to be playing an exhibition game against a team from one of the nearby counties. They're supposed to be really good, and Coach Blackburn wants to see me pitch against them. He said there should be a good crowd on hand, probably even some scouts. There's a lot on the line. It could all come down to this one game. I talked to your mother about it first, and she gave the go ahead. So, your aunt can help by looking after your mom and you can come watch the game. Would you like that?"

"Yeah." Jake's excitement was genuine, even though he already knew about the game and what was at stake. "When's the game going to be played?"

"The day after tomorrow." His father fist-bumped Jake's shoulder. "Come on. Let's get some sleep. We'll need all the energy we can muster to beat this team."

Jake went to his room, but he had his mind set on talking with Lorcan. He waited until the house was quiet and he was sure that his father was asleep, then he snuck out of his bedroom and tiptoed downstairs. He searched the kitchen for something sweet for Lorcan, but his mother didn't leave very much behind. He managed to find almost a full slice of bread and dribbled some honey on it. That would have to do, he thought.

He placed the sticky treat on the landing at the bottom of the stairs like he did the night before to attract Lorcan. He didn't think the goblin would appear while he was there watching, so instead of going back up to his room to wait, he decided to investigate the basement. He didn't know what he was looking for or what he would find as he removed several moth-eaten blankets. He uncovered a set of pine ladderback chairs, a butterfly table, candlestands, and other early colonial American furnishings. They seemed to be just the kinds of things that would be of interest to his aunt. Columns of dust drifted into the air and fell back down over his face, initiating a sneezing fit that he didn't think would ever stop. When it finally did, he held his breath and waited for another episode to pass.

"Achoooo!"

This sneeze was exaggerated and wet, but it did not come from him. It originated from a low shelf somewhere along the far wall. Jake walked over and saw Lorcan reclined on a pile of old newspapers. He was holding a finger under his nose, his eyes closed tightly and his mouth hanging open.

"A-a-a-achooooo!"

This one was even wetter and more protracted. The turbulence from the goblin's explosive sneeze disturbed a cloud of dust that drifted in front of Jake's face and made him sneeze too.

"Hey, come on," Jake protested.

"I can't help it," Lorcan said defensively, his voice nasally, his nose dripping. "You started it."

Jake took a step back, waving an open hand in front of his face to brush away the lingering dust. "What are you doing down here?"

The goblin wiped his nose with the back of his hand then licked it off. "I came down to get away from that woman."

"My aunt? Did she see you?"

"I think so. She followed me down here, but I hid behind some boxes. After I while…" He shrugged his shoulders. "I got sleepy."

Jake noticed that Lorcan's mouth was ringed with dried bubble gum. "What's that on your face?"

"Where?"

"There. On your lips." Jake reached out to touch it but Lorcan pulled away. "It's bubble gum," he said in an accusatory tone. "*My* bubble gum. You were in my room last night, weren't you?"

Lorcan bowed his head and nodded slowly.

"You were looking for the Sacred Amulet to give to Buach?"

"No, no. I was…I was…I was looking for bubble gum."

"What? Bubble gum? Why?"

"I like bubble gum." The goblin stuck his hands into the pockets of his trousers to show Jake that they were filled with gum. "A lot."

"My room was all torn apart. The gum was in a bucket on top of my desk. Why did you wreck my room?"

"Well, I was chewing the gum and I started reading your baseball books while you were sleeping. I was so absorbed by all that analytical stuff that I lost track of time. The next thing I knew, it was almost dawn and I had to leave. I didn't have time to straighten out the mess I made. I'm Sorry."

"You like sabermetrics?" Jake's voice rose so high it cracked.

Lorcan nodded. "I do, even though I don't understand a lot of it. I'd like to know more. Maybe you can explain it to me better. In exchange, I can tell you more about the true history of baseball. Your books don't talk about how it *really* began."

"They don't?"

Lorcan told him about how the Tisdales made changes to a game played in England and Ireland called Rounders, and how these changes eventually became American baseball.

"This very spot is where the modern game of baseball originated," Lorcan said, raising his chin with pride. "That's why I've devoted my existence to this house and whoever occupies it."

"Wow." Jake didn't know what else to say. It was incredible, but he believed what Lorcan told him.

"Did you know that goblins are forbidden from playing with humans," Lorcan teased. "Over the years, however, a couple of goblins are believed to have snuck into the Major Leagues, including Mordecai "Three Finger" Brown, a pitcher from a hundred years ago who was thought to be a brownie. And today, some say Aaron Judge is really a golem."

Jake was completely enthralled by what Lorcan told him about the hidden history of baseball. He listened to more of Lorcan's stories, and he explained the basics of sabermetrics to the goblin in return. They talked for hours. When Jake finally went up to his room, the first rays of sunlight could be seen behind the trees along the eastern border of the Adirondacks.

Bottom of the 6th

It was exactly where he left it all those years ago. Buach hadn't opened the box since he placed his baseball mitt there after taking it off his hand the last time, he wore it. As he eased his left hand into the glove, his lips parted slightly, which was the closest thing that the evil goblin had come to a genuine smile in a long time. The brown cowhide had darkened over time, and it was dry and cracking in a few places, but it still fit. He smacked his fist into the pocket. It made a loud POP and dust exploded from it upon impact. It felt good too.

The Overlord opened and closed his glove several times to loosen the stiff leather. He had made the glove with his own hands. There was substantial webbing between the thumb and first finger, creating a pre-formed pocket. He came up with this original design long before William Leopold Doak got all the credit for this improvement. "Spittin' Bill" showed the design to an equipment manufacturer which began to mass produce the glove. Soon, this new glove design replaced all baseball gloves of the time, and it remains the standard to this day.

Buach never gave it much thought that he did something that has had a profound influence on the game played by humans. He blocked it out of his mind. He blocked everything that had to do with baseball out of his mind. He displaced *all* fond thoughts he had about the game. Anytime the topic of baseball came up, he became filled with blind rage. It fueled his vengeful fury. Baseball begot anger, and the anger only made him hate baseball more. He was tormented by this internal conflict, which transformed a once friendly, if mischievous goblin, into the most malicious creature the goblin kingdom has ever known. It changed a goblin who wanted nothing more than to play baseball every day into a self-imposed tyrant who wanted to banish the game forever.

Buach didn't think he would ever play baseball again. Having to play again now made him intensely angry, but he had been challenged, and he couldn't refuse to play. A victory over the Resistance meant consolidation of his power, and nothing mattered more than that to him.

Seething, he went to join the other members of the Order, who were practicing for the big game. The field abound with rambunctious goblins, sliding on the infield dirt, laughing, and enjoying themselves as they tossed and batted baseballs to one another. Buach stepped over the first base line near home plate, careful to raise his tail so as not to disturb the chalk and came to a halt. His presence instantly brought dark clouds across the cobalt blue sky, obscuring the sun. The wind began to whip up and the air temperature dropped twenty degrees.

"ALL RIGHT, THAT'S ENOUGH!" Buach shouted.

They all stopped what they were doing, falling still and silent.

"We were just having a little fun," said Fergus, a two feet tall knocker wearing the clothes of a miner.

"Yeah, we'll destroy those goblins in the Resistance," said one of the kobolds clustered in a group near second base.

"Easily," added another. The front of his jersey was dirty from practicing headfirst slides.

"I don't want to see anymore fooling around." This command was followed by a crack of thunder. If he didn't have every goblin's complete and undivided attention before, he had it now. They all knew what Buach was capable of doing, especially when he was angry, but such a display of power was always a good reminder.

"We have to take this game serious," Buach lectured. "We don't want to just beat them. We want to destroy them. Embarrass them. We have to be at the top of our game. You were all great players once, but it's been a long time since any of us last played. And we don't have a lot of time to practice. Now, let's get to work."

He began calling out the positions he wanted the goblins to play, instructing the others to get their bats.

"Who's going to pitch?" asked Finbar. The trow's voice was faint.

"I am," Buach sneered. "Why don't you put the catching gear on first."

Finbar hitched in place. He didn't like what putting on the catching gear 'first' implied, but he did what he was told. Trows were the most obedient of all the creatures in Pine Barrows, and Buach counted on them. Finbar's shoulders slumped as he walked to the dugout to put on the equipment.

"Let's see what we can do in a game situation," the Overlord said. Before throwing his first pitch, he moved Fergus, who was playing shortstop, to the other side of second base.

"Why are you putting me here?" the knocker inquired, scratching his head. "There's a big hole between short and third now."

"These goblins aren't going to get around on my fastball." Buach puffed out his chest. "If they hit the ball at all, it's going to be to the opposite side."

Buach didn't know that this simple defensive shift was part of the sabermetrics movement that has swept through baseball in the human world. However, he understood that historical knowledge of a player's strengths and weaknesses could affect not only the outcome of a single at-bat, but ultimately impact who wins the game.

"Okay, let's look alive out here," he told his defense and then anchored both feet on the pitching rubber. At that moment, Buach experienced a sense of power and control that was even more pervasive than that of being Overlord.

Finbar was crouched down behind the plate, his hand shaking as he held up a rudimentary catcher's mitt fashioned out of a burlap bag stuffed with sheep wool. As Einin dug into the right-hand batter's box, Finbar put down one finger. Buach acknowledged the sign and went into his wind-up, a herky-jerky motion that looked more like performance art than a pitching motion. He had a high leg kick, extending his foot out in front of him, while his torso bent back in the opposite direction. It looked like he might fall over, but he used his tale to balance himself until he delivered the pitch. With so much going on, it was hard for the batter to pick up the ball. By the time he did, it was too late. Einin didn't have a chance. He didn't even get the bat off his shoulders as Buach plus-fastball whizzed by him at 110 miles per hour.

Finbar held his mitt in place to receive the ball and closed his eyes. The trow was knocked off his feet and thrown all the way to the backstop by the force of the impact. Finbar held his broken hand against his belly and screeched in pain. He had to be helped off the field.

Buach smirked, satisfied with the pitch, particularly considering that it was the first time he had thrown a baseball in a very long time. He looked in the dugout. "All right, Peadar, put the catching gear on." The bogey was small, but solidly built, much more sturdy than Finbar. Buach had used the trow to show just how important this game was and that he meant business. The point was not missed by any of the goblins, least of all Finbar, who was being attended to in the dugout by Turlough, the oldest member of the team and the only tengu, a humanoid with bird-like features. Turlough, who fancied himself a healer, applied some willow bark to the trow's injured hand and then wrapped it in cloth bandages to suppress the swelling.

Buach pitched only one inning, but it was all he needed. He was happy with his control and the command he had of his pitches. He was also satisfied with how comfortable he felt on the mound.

The Overlord worked his players hard. By the end of practice, it was clear that they had tremendous ability and could easily beat any team, human or goblin. They made every play in the field and hit homerun after homerun deep into the woods. These goblins certainly knew they were far superior to any group of goblins the Mound Men would field. However, as cocky and sure of themselves as the players were, Buach refused to take anything for granted. He was confident that he could keep his goblins focused, which was all that it would take to ensure victory.

In the back of his mind, however, there was one thing that really worried him; his goblins seemed to have too much fun playing baseball again. He witnessed their enjoyment with his own eyes. As much as he wished it were not the case, they clearly loved being out there, not just playing the game but relishing in the shared camaraderie. As for Buach himself, he could not deny that he had fun out there, as well.

So, that made two things that worried him.

With the source of his power, as well as the Order's successful takeover of Pine Barrows, wholly dependent on the complete banishment of baseball, just playing this game against Skip's team seemed at odds with what he was trying to accomplish.

Buach had to acknowledge that this might be part of a larger plan cooked up by Skip Blackburn. If that were the case, and it was all a trap, then he had to make sure that the game was no fun for his players. This, in turn, made him wonder if it was even possible to play the game of baseball and not have fun. Even losing did not diminish the fun of playing the game, which you played as hard as you could until the very last out was made because in baseball anything could happen.

Anything could happen.

That was another thing that worried him.

Top of the 7th

He had gone through the goblin portal, navigated down the dark tunnel under the field and emerged in the dugout, met first by an explosion of sunlight that temporarily blinded him. The field was absolutely alive with goblins talking and laughing. As his eyes adjusted to the brightness, he saw that a scrimmage was in progress, the team preparing for the game against the Order. The infielders were joking with the runners that were on base. It was a stark contrast to how the goblins on Buach's team were getting ready for the upcoming matchup.

The bases were loaded, and the catcher, Thorn Pepperstaff, was on the mound with his mask pulled up on top of his head, talking with his father. The kobold was nicknamed Slash because he had a penchant for bunting. Although he was a good catcher, he could not hit very well. But he was extremely fast, so when he laid down a bunt, he often beat it out. Sometimes, when the infield came way in, he would square around like he was going to bunt and then he would pull his bat back and swing at the pitch, only occasionally hitting it hard enough to get it by the infielders.

Skip was shouting to the goblin catcher from the top step of the dugout. Slash nodded, said something through his catcher's mitt to his father, and lowered the mask back over his face before trotting back behind the plate.

"Skip, I need to talk to you." Jake walked by several goblins who were cheering from their seats in the dugout.

Skip waved a hand dismissively behind his back. "I want to see how he gets out of this jam," the goblin manager said as he studied his father's every movement and expression. "I put him in just now with the bases loaded, nobody out, and everything on the line."

"You owe me an explanation," Jake demanded.

Skip's attention remained on the field.

"I talked to Ruadhan."

The manager suddenly turned around, eyes wide, mouth agape. Behind him, his father threw a fastball that the goblin hitter swung through for a strike.

"He told me everything." Jake walked up to Skip and stopped directly in front of him. "Including that he was under instruction from you, not Buach. You had him give my mother to that demon."

"It was the only way," Skip said in a measured tone.

"She might not come back." Jake's voice rose with emotion, unsteady and cracking.

"It was done for your own well-being." The goblin manager placed a hand on Jake's shoulder, like his father would do sometimes. "Buach's darkness is a threat not only to you and your family and the goblins who live in Pine Barrows, but to every living creature everywhere, human and goblin. That's all I can say about that for now. You have to trust me."

The funny thing was, he did trust Skip. He wasn't sure why, but he did. Jake and his family had a dog for a short time, and he remembered how the animal would look at him in such a way that he knew the dog would never hurt him. Skip looked at him the same way.

"There is something that you should know about the outcome of this game," Skip went on to say. "If we win, your mom will be freed from the goblin kingdom. However, according to goblin rules, another human would have to take her place."

Jake knew exactly what that meant. "Me," he said.

The goblin manager nodded.

"But winning saves my mom, Pine Barrows, and all the goblins imprisoned by Buach?"

"And baseball," Skip added.

None of the information explained why his mother had to be taken in the first place. Jake supposed it didn't really matter at the moment. If the Mound Men lost, everything was lost.

"There's something else you don't know." The goblin manager's eyes were stern. "The goblins playing for Buach are all exceptionally good players."

"So are the Mound Men."

"If you think my players are good, wait until you see these guys." Skip offered a humorless smile. "And none are better than Buach himself. He can do it all. Hit, pitch, field, run."

"Wait a minute. You said you cut Buach from your team."

"Buach wasn't cut because of how he played. There was only one thing he couldn't do; he was not a team player. It was all about him. He refused to bunt or give himself up in any situation, and he wouldn't hit a ball the other way to move a runner over. He would wait for the perfect pitch and try to hit a home run. He wouldn't swing if he didn't get the pitch he wanted. Because of these things, he didn't get along with his teammates, which created a lot of hostility and tension in the dugout. Despite being the best player on the field, he made every team he played on worse."

Jake nodded with newfound understanding, and hope. "You think the Order can be beaten, then?"

Skip hitched his shoulders and raised his eyebrows. "It's not going to be easy," he conceded. "Buach is virtually unhittable if he has his stuff." The goblin manager turned toward the field. Jake followed his gaze. They both watched as his father dropped a backdoor curveball that completely fooled a left-handed hitter.

"Steeeeeee-rike three!" the umpire intoned. The goblin official looked like a large tortoise with its shell turned around, its tiny head peeking out the top. The frustrated goblin batter slammed his bat against the ground with such force that it shattered in a thousand pieces.

"How could you even see the ball?" the batter yelled at the ump. "Your head was in your shell when he threw it." He lumbered back to the other dugout, mumbling to himself.

"Two down," the shortstop yelled out to his teammates on the field, holding up two of the three fingers he had on his hand.

Skip looked back at Jake. "The way your dad has been pitching, we have a chance."

"With Buach being as good as you say, even if my father could match him pitch for pitch, we still have to steal at least one run to win."

The goblin manager nodded. "If this game teaches us anything, it is that anything can happen in baseball. At any moment, of any game, you might see something that has never been witnessed before. That's baseball. That's life."

Jake looked out across a baseball field that was populated with goblins. "That's for sure."

"The only thing that would ensure a victory for the Order would be possessing the Sacred Amulet," Skip said. "Its power is supreme. It would guarantee victory for anyone who possesses it. That's why Buach continues his steadfast hunt for it, even at this moment."

"Lorcan won't give the Sacred Amulet to the Order if he finds it. Don't worry."

"Bless little Lorcan," Skip said with a smile. "He is an honorable goblin, but he has put himself in grave danger."

"You think Buach will hurt Lorcan?"

"With everything that's on the line in this game, you can bet that Buach will stop at nothing to ensure that the Order comes out on top."

Behind them, the inning concluded with a called third strike. As his father walked off the mound, he shrugged his right shoulder. The motion was almost imperceptible, but Skip noticed it and called him over.

"That was a high-pressure situation," the goblin coach told him. "Didn't look like it bothered you at all. Great job. How's the shoulder feel?"

"It started to tighten up a little during that last sequence," his father disclosed. "But it's nothing. I'm fine."

"All right. That's it for today anyway. Some of the other pitchers need some work. Ice that shoulder and take it easy. You're ready for the game."

"Thanks, coach." He walked away, swiveling his head around, keeping a cautious eye out for Prank.

It was a strange to observe his father this way. Jake felt like he was spying on him. "Skip, my Dad can't see me *at all?*"

"Nope. To him, you could be a stick lying on the ground or a wad of gum."

"He can't hear me, either?"

"A stick or wad of gum can't talk."

Several of the goblin players came over to see Jake. Prank lifted him up, balancing the boy on his head as he turned all around with a look of mock confusion.

"Where did he go?" Prank asked. "Did anybody see where that human boy went. He was here a minute ago."

"Put him down," Skip demanded.

"Put *who* down?"

"Cut it out, Prank." Skip turned his attention to the rest of his players. "Lupo's done for today. Who wants to pitch?" He looked directly up at Jake. "How about you?"

"Me?" Jake almost fell off the goblin's head.

"Sure. Get out there and throw the old leather."

"But I can't pitch."

Prank pulled Jake off his shoulders and set him gently on the ground. "That's a great idea, Skip," he said.

"I haven't even thrown my fifty pitches today," Jake protested.

"It's just a scrimmage game," Prank added. He carried the boy out of the dugout and placed him on the mound." It's baseball. It's fun."

"I didn't bring my glove."

"You can borrow mine." Prank handed his glove to Jake, who looked it over carefully to be sure there was no ketchup or mayonnaise or spiders inside of it. "I'm leading off the inning. Let's see what you got, kid." He went to retrieve his baseball bat as a group of goblins took the field.

Slash squatted down behind home plate and smacked his mitt. "Throw a couple of warmups."

Jake scooped up the ball that was lying beside the rubber. He held it in his hand, spinning it around in his palm. Until that moment, he was unsure of himself, but as soon as his fingers found the seams on the ball, he knew he could do it. He glanced over at Skip on the top step of the dugout. The goblin manager smiled and gave him a wink.

Prank dug into the batter's box, his right foot carving out a deep hole. He waved his bat in sharp concentric loops over his head, and his hips swiveled back and forth in anticipation of the pitch. To call it a batting stance was a contradiction because his body was in constant motion.

Slash called for a fastball away. Jake nodded and went into his windup, focused only on the mitt. His pitch hit the exact spot where the catcher had set up. Prank watched it go by and the umpire called it a strike.

"Great pitch, kid," Slash said.

The catcher called for a breaking ball next, setting up on inner third of the plate. Jake delivered what he thought was likely the best curveball he had ever thrown. It broke a foot and backed Prank off the plate before dropping over for strike two.

"Nice hook, kid." Slash tossed the ball back to Jake. "One more."

This time the catcher called for a changeup. Jake wanted to shake it off. It was a pitch he was not comfortable throwing because he couldn't control it. It usually stayed up in the zone and just sort of floated. He didn't want to second-guess his batterymate, so he nodded in agreement. As soon as the ball left his hand, he knew it was a mistake. Prank took a mighty swing and the ball rocketed off his bat. It sailed high above the tree line, still increasing in height as it left the field. Prank watched it until it was out of sight before he dropped his bat. Instead of jogging to first base, he headed to third, rounding the bases in reverse. The other goblins booed him, and the infielders tossed their gloves at him as he passed by them.

Jake stood slump-shouldered on the mound. Skip went out to have a word with him after Prank crossed home plate.

"Don't let that *prima donna* get to you," the goblin manager told him.

"I told you I can't pitch." Jake slammed the glove against the ground and ran off into the dugout. Before he could reach the door at the far end, Bud Reedtwist, a thickly muscled goblin, grabbed him by the shirttail and held him in place.

"Let go of me," Jake demanded.

"Where are you going?" Bud asked in a raspy, toneless voice. "Coach wasn't through talking to you."

"I don't care. Let me go." His shirt was starting to tear when Skip arrived. Jake settled down and Skip dismissed the goblin detaining him.

"You have to get back out there," Skip said. "Finish the inning."

"I'm never going to pitch again. Ever."

"You can't make a decision like that based on this one outcome. You have a plus-fastball and an out-of-this-world curveball. And it was me who called for that changeup. When thrown properly, a changeup is a deadly weapon. It reaches the plate between 10-15% slower than your fastball, with both arm-side run and sink. If you can make it appear to the batter that you're about to throw a fastball, the change in speed and placement of the ball will make the pitch practically unhittable." Skip smiled. "All you have to do is work a little on the grip and mechanics. I can help you with that."

What the goblin manager said made sense to Jake, but it did little to ease his frustration and disappointment. He thought about his mother. They had to win this game.

"I suppose there will be plenty of time for me to practice when I'm in the goblin world." Jake lowered his head and moved toward the tunnel under the field. He had to get home to warn Lorcan and find the Sacred Amulet before the Order got their hands on it.

After Jake left, Skip smiled again. It was a smile that was not meant for the boy to see.

Bottom of the 7th

The old cart creaked, and its contents jangled as she pushed the wooden wheelbarrow across the back of the yard as quickly and as quietly as she could. She did not want to be seen or heard as she headed off to the forest with the goods. Once beyond the tree line, she slowed her pace, searching the forest floor for specific plants. When she found the ones she was looking for, she pulled them out of the ground by the root. She spotted the deep yellow and orange flowers of the pleurisy plant first, followed by black cohosh, a flowering herbal plant which was a member of the buttercup family. The hardest to come by, but the easiest to spot, was unicorn root, which grew in long spikes, its stem covered in small, white tubular flowers.

Briget knew she was being watched as she deposited the medicinal plants into the pockets of her blouse.

"Jenny'll get you," a raspy, gurgling voice said.

She looked around at the trees and the nearby body of water. The pond was still and appeared empty but standing at the edge of the water amid floating vegetation and rotting tree stumps was a long-limbed woman whose skin was olive green. She had long slimy hair, like wet lichen covering her naked body.

"You have something for Jenny?" The water hag opened her mouth wide as she spoke, revealing tiny, sharp teeth. "Jenny's got something for you. Come a little closer, deary."

"No," Briget shouted defiantly and pushed her collection of antiques deeper into the woods, far away from the pond.

"Jenny'll get you," the voice repeated, growing fainter until she was out of earshot.

Briget stopped beside a cluster of three trees with low canopies like an umbrella. Buach only allowed his red, glaring eyes to be visible to her, and she didn't notice his approach until he was upon her. She gave a startled yelp when she saw the flaming orbs floating in the preternatural darkness under the thorn trees.

"Are you the one they call Buach?" she calmly asked.

The Overlord had no intention of presenting any more of himself to the human. "Who are you and why are you in my woods?" His voice echoed as if in a cave.

"I'm a relic hunter," Briget said. "I find and trade powerful relics and treasure that humans discard and exchange them with goblins for power."

Buach's eyes dimmed slightly as if squinting with introspection. "How did you find me?"

"I was given the temporary power to see all goblins by Brin, leader of a goblin troupe in the Black Hills. I bestowed him with silver and gold, and he told me of a great goblin ruler in Pine Barrows who could use my services. Do you know Brin?"

The Overlord only snarled, a low angry growl that Briget ignored.

She sifted through the assortment of wooden tools and ceramic and porcelain crockery, presenting an amphora and a washboard with ribbed glass to Buach. "What do you think of these items?" she asked, smiling with more zeal than seemed appropriate.

"Junk," he erupted. "Useless junk."

"How about something smaller." She dug out an old perfume bottle and a hand-carved wooden Christmas ornament, holding the objects up for his inspection.

"These things mean nothing to me." Buach's eyes blazed.

Briget continued searching the trove, disregarding his growing irritation. "Wait," she began. "I was told by Brin that you were in search of a particular item of great value. He informed me that you sought a secret omelet-maker."

"Secret Omelet-maker?"

"To make a secret omelet, I suspect. But that's none of my business. Now, I couldn't find that, exactly, but I do have a nice antique waffle-maker." She rummaged through the wheelbarrow in search of the item. "I know it's in here somewhere…Oh, I got it," she announced triumphantly, raising it up. "It's a little rusty, but it works fine."

"It's the *Sacred Amulet* that I seek." He was seething.

"Hmmm. I don't think I have that. What does it look like?"

Buach roared loudly. The reverberations shook the trees and rattled the items in Briget's cart.

"So, you don't want this?" She waved the appliance in front of Buach's eyes. "You can make crepes with this, too."

The Overlord did not respond to her.

"Oh, I know." She unceremoniously dropped the waffle-maker into the wheelbarrow and pulled out a small cloth sack.

She grinned as she loosened the drawstring and opened the top to reveal a cache of coins and gems that glittered in the light reflected from Buach's fire-eyes. "Surely, you can give me something for this," she continued. "Grant me just a small extension of power."

A force, like an invisible hand, knocked the sack out of her grasp. The sack struck the ground, its contents of broken glass, rat skulls, and beetles spilling out onto the damp forest floor.

"Do you think you can fool me with such tricks?" His voice thundered. "You have insulted the Great Buach."

"I apologize. I'm a businesswoman. Just tell me what you need, and I will bring it to you. I have a lot more stuff I can show you. You wouldn't believe how much is in that old farmhouse."

"Do not come back unless you have the Sacred Amulet for me. If I catch you in these woods without it, you will meet a grim end at the hands of a very ornery red cap." The fire in his eyes flickered momentarily and then just extinguished. "Be gone!" his disembodied voice commanded.

She gathered the worthless treasure up off the ground, putting everything back into the sack except for the beetles, which scurried off and disappeared beneath the carpet of decaying leaves. She turned the wheelbarrow around and pushed it forward out of the woods.

Buach could still see her. He watched her until the forest consumed her. The visual made him grin. If she could get her hands on the Sacred Amulet, the time and aggravation that the encounter with the human woman cost him would have been all worthwhile. At least it would not fall into Skip's hands and be used by the Resistance. Even if the relic hunter failed to find it, the advantage remained in the Order's favor. He would deal with her himself after the game. He didn't want the red cap to have all the fun. But Lorcan needed to be dealt with first. The hogboon had outlived his usefulness. The Overlord laughed with delight at the thought as he set out to locate Flann and sanction the red cap to dispose of Lorcan.

Briget heard the laughter but did not look back. The items she brought the goblin Overlord did not impress him in the least. This told her a couple of things. The first was that the Sacred Amulet he sought was extremely valuable. The second was that its value was perhaps even greater to other goblin leaders. It could be traded for a great deal of power to the right goblin. Power that would exceed what even her sister possessed. She suppressed her own laughter at this thought, knowing that she was likely being watched and she had to be careful with this Buach. He was not deceived by the broken glass. His power was very strong, indeed.

On her way back to the folk house, there were numerous holes she steered the wheelbarrow around. Many were sufficiently large, and she chose one near the edge of the property to dump the load of useless items inside. The stuff filled it almost to the top. She kicked in just enough dirt to conceal it all and left the wheelbarrow near the backdoor of the folk house.

She paused to look up the second floor bedroom window where her sister was laid up in bed. She wasn't sure what was wrong with Erin, but she suspected that the condition might involve early menopause. She wanted to help her sister, and the roots of the plants she collected, when combined properly, were supposed to help alleviate the symptoms of the condition.

Though the two women were sisters, Briget was adopted, so she did not share the goblin blood that ran through Erin's veins. Briget did not think it was fair. To make it worse, her sister never took advantage of this power. Briget yearned for all the benefits that goblin DNA would bestow upon her. She would not have denied herself the full benefits of this birthright the way her sister had, and she was determined to accumulate her own power by whatever means necessary, including trading gold and silver and other relics for it.

But something didn't feel right. She hadn't spoken to her sister in five years, and when she showed up at her doorstep unexpectedly, it was as if Erin didn't remember that there was bad blood between them. Her sister's odd behavior raised many questions. Briget wondered why Erin would pretend that everything was fine. If it were a trick, she couldn't figure out the angle. The only thing she could think of was that Erin was trying to lay a guilt-trip on her to get her to apologize. That, Briget resolved, wasn't going to happen.

What her sister didn't understood was that it was never about their parents' house and possessions alone, including the gold and silver coins. Their value was so much higher in her hands because of the power she could acquire with it. Her sister didn't need the coins because she already had power, even if she chose not to use it.

As it turned out, the coins held even more value because they belonged to a family with traces of goblin blood in their lineage. The silver and gold pieces fetched a lot more than she thought they would. She had taken them to numerous goblin rulers in exchange for power, trading a few of them at a time to maximize the return that they would bring to her. Several goblin leaders wanted to take all the coins from her, but they were not willing to give her something that she wanted more than anything, which was to be welcomed into the goblin world as one of their own.

Collectively, the coins had given her considerable power, but it was temporary, and she remained a long way from achieving her goal. Now, she was out of coins and she was desperate.

Briget dared to consider that maybe her sister just wanted to put their family problems behind them for good. The condition that Erin was suffering from may very well have been the motivation behind her rethinking their relationship. Perhaps Erin was even considering sharing some of her power. Of course, it could just as easily be a trap. She would have to be on the lookout for that, and anything else that left her vulnerable.

Just as this thought played on her mind, she saw something that stopped her in her tracks. The thickset goblin looked like a gruesome old man with greenish skin, long teeth set in its lower jaw, and wispy white hair streaming down to its shoulders. It was carrying a pikestaff and wore iron boots on its feet and a distinctive red cap atop its head.

It stalked away from the house and down the driveway toward the road. Briget just stared, terrified but unable to look away. It was rare for any human to get a glimpse of this goblin, but it was even more extraordinary to see it outside the safety of the forest in the middle of the day, where its kind seldom, if ever, ventured.

Briget did not understand what she was seeing. Perhaps the creature had special powers to be where it was, but it did not make her feel safe.

Top of the 8th

Jake got home before his father, and the house was deathly silent. While the stick that passed as his mother was resting soundly in bed, his aunt was nowhere to be found, and neither was Lorcan. He worried that Buach had imprisoned his little friend. Or worse. He didn't want to think about that.

He paused at the bottom of the stairs, wondering where to even begin searching for the magic object. There was little time and few opportunities remaining to find the Sacred Amulet. Now it seemed that he would have to do it without Lorcan's help.

Movement outside the living room window drew Jake's attention. He recognized the forbidding figure instantly as Flann, the red cap he had encountered at the field with Buach. The murderous goblin strode casually up the driveway toward the road, the low sun glinting off the blade of its pikestaff.

Jake was surprised to see Flann out in the open, so far from the woods. Even when Jake caught glimpses of goblins prior to moving to Pine Barrows, they were always in the woods, and they always appeared after dusk.

The front door suddenly opened. He jumped, but his aunt didn't seem surprised to see him standing there. Judging by her calm demeanor, he guessed she had not seen the frightful goblin outside the farmhouse.

"Hi, Aunt Briget."

"Hello, Jake. I was just out collecting these." She pulled the flowering plants from her pockets.

"What's all that?"

"Herbs and roots." She held them out in one grouping, a colorful visual array. "I have some black cohosh, pleurisy root and some unicorn root."

"Unicorn?"

"Not unicorn, as in the mythical animal," she said with a little laugh. "Although this home remedy is pretty magical. There is quite a variety of medicinal plants native to this region."

"You mean, it's medicine?"

"It will be once I mix up these ingredients and add a tiny bit of alcohol. It's an old folk remedy. The compound derived from these ingredients should have your mom feeling better in no time. You want to help me prepare the tincture?"

"Sure," Jake agreed. They went into the kitchen and he watched her lay out several cloth bags and run the plants under some water in the sink. "What are you doing?" he asked her.

"It's called maceration," his aunt said. "I'm steeping the plants, soaking them, to soften them up."

"How do you know how to do all this?"

"I'm a bit of an herbalist," she confessed. "In my line of work, I meet a lot of people who not only have a lot of old things, but a lot of old ways of doing things. I picked up a few of these remedies along the way."

She described what she was doing and why, and Jake helped her combine the wet plants and place them in a cloth bag.

She added a little alcohol to preserve the mixture and then filtered it through another cloth before pouring it into a glass.

Jake sniffed the concoction and wrinkled his nose. "It stinks," he said. "Is this really going to work?"

"Should fix her up, just like that." She snapped her fingers. "Come on. Let's go give it to her."

They left the kitchen and were on their way to the staircase when Jake's father walked in holding something against his right shoulder.

"Dad!" He ran over to his father's side. "What's that?" he asked with breathless concern.

His father removed the checked cloth bag and shook it. Melted ice sloshed around inside. It had a screw-on aluminum cap. "This is what they called an ice pack a hundred years ago."

"What happened to your shoulder?"

"Nothing." He flexed the shoulder, raising it up and down. "See." He mimed throwing a pitch. "I'm fine. I had a final tune-up this afternoon and I really let it fly. I just wanted to ice it down to be sure I'm 100% for the game tomorrow."

"You will be," Jake assured him.

"Thanks, sport. How's your mom doing?"

"We were just on our way up to see her," Aunt Briget informed him. "Why don't we all go up together."

Jake took the ice pack from his father and examined it. "A hundred years old," he said, then looked up at his aunt. "Is this an antique, Aunt Briget?"

She laughed. "That's one of those items that doesn't have any value to *anybody*."

"I don't know about that," Jake's father said. "The Mound Men have hundreds of these things."

Jake didn't want to go up with them, but his father put his hand on his back and guided him into his mother's room. She was sitting up in bed, staring directly at him. He looked away. His aunt stood on one side of the bed, his father on the other side. Although he could hear them speaking, he wasn't listening to what they were saying. His mother's eyes remained locked on him, and she was smiling with her lips closed. She lifted her arms, extending them toward him. Her fingers made a sound like creaking wood as she beckoned him.

"Jake, come and see your mother," his father instructed.

Jake looked up at his father with wide eyes, his feet firmly planted on the floor.

She's not my mom, she's not my mom.

His father stepped over to him and he felt the touch of his father's large hand on the back of his neck. "There's nothing to be afraid of. Give your mom a hug."

Jake was unable to oppose the forceful nudge that compelled him over to his mother's bedside. He needed a final push to get close enough to her so she could put her arms around him. She drew him in close. He could feel her arms like tree branches embracing him, her fingers like twigs digging into his skin. She smelled like wet leaves.

"You are my sunshine, my only sunshine, you make me happy when skies are gray," she sang softly. "You'll never know dear, how much I love you. So please, don't take my sunshine away..."

She's not my mom, she's not my mom.

"...The other night dear, as I lay sleeping, I dreamed I held you in my arms, but when I awoke, dear, I was mistaken."

Jake pulled away briskly, cutting his cheek on her rough bark/skin in the process.

"I miss you, son," she said.

A shiver ran down his spine. She never called him, *son.* This replica of his mother didn't seem to know who he was. He noticed that the small freckle she had on the left side of her neck now had the appearance of a small knot in a tree.

"I miss my mom, too," he responded.

She just smiled. Her lips parted, revealing wooden teeth.

"I have something for you, Erin." Aunt Briget held out the glass of medicine she made from the plants she picked in the woods.

"I hope you have more than that to offer me," his mother told her. "I'm starving."

"This is a mild tonic to start you off," his aunt said. "It will help you feel better. We'll get something heartier for you to eat after you take this."

Jake saw his mother's skin fossilize before his eyes, turning into smooth, ashen bark. His father and his aunt did not see her transform into a branch. They just continued their conversation about food. He took advantage of this distraction and left the room without looking back. Closing the door behind him, he paused in the hallway, resting his back against the wall and breathing deeply. He interpreted what he had just seen as a sure sign that there was very little time left for his mother. The game had to be played and won to stop the transformation from being complete.

His father came out of the room alone and stood beside him. "Hi, sport," his father began. "I know it's hard seeing your mother the way she is right now, but she really needs you. She needs all of us. Your aunt's arrival seems to have helped a lot. Maybe that herbal remedy will do some good, too, who knows. But even though your mother seems to have perked up a little recently, she doesn't seem to be getting any better."

"What are you trying to say, Dad?"

"Well, after the exhibition game tomorrow, we'll be going back to the city. I already told Skip."

"I understand," Jake said. "Can I still come and watch?"

"I can do you one better than that. They're looking for a bat boy. The job is yours. If you want it."

"Yes. Do I get one of those jerseys with the "BB" on it."

"I think that can be arranged. It'll be a lot of fun. And however, this game goes for me, at least I'll know if I have what it takes or not."

"If you can beat this team, Dad, you can play for any Major League team."

His father smiled. "You really think so?"

"I *know* so."

"The confidence you have in me means everything. You should have the same confidence in yourself that I have in you. Now let's go fix us all something to eat. I bought some good carbohydrate-rich foods at the farm-stand. I tell you all the time how important proper nutrition is for optimal sports performance."

"Can you carry me downstairs over your shoulder like a fireman the way you used to."

"I don't know. You're not a little kid anymore, but I'll try." He lifted Jake up and tossed him over his left shoulder instead of his right "Boy, have you gotten heavy since the last time I did this."

Jake saw his father wince as he lifted him, but once he was up, his father's legs were sturdy enough to carry him down without a problem. A pitcher had to have strong legs, and his father's legs were plenty strong.

"Wait 'til I tell you what Prank did today," his father said as he placed Jake down on the floor in the kitchen. "It was really funny. Especially because he did it to someone else and not me for a change."

"What did he do?"

"Help me bring the shopping inside and I'll tell you as we get supper ready."

There were five paper bags on the porch filled with potatoes, apples, carrots, oranges, bananas, eggs, milk, and peanut butter.

Jake was encouraged by his father's enthusiasm and how prepared he was to give the Mound Men his best pitching performance. Without the Sacred Amulet, he hoped it would be enough.

Bottom of the 8th

This time she walked into the woods carrying only one small item in a cloth napkin. Her purpose for being there was as different as her offering. If Buach would not meet her, she would find someone who could get her into his lair. She didn't know who was watching her, or whose attention she would attract, but she avoided the pond. She wanted no part of Jenny Greenteeth.

The forest was darker and colder than Briget remembered it, another sign that any power she had been previously gifted by the goblins in exchange for gold and silver was all but exhausted.

Determined to make a deal with a goblin who could lead her to Buach, she wandered further into the woods than she intended. She got a whiff of death and decay before she saw anything. Then she entered an expanse of land that had been completely decimated. Trees were scarred and broken, the ground violently trampled. It looked as if a herd of wild elephants had rampaged through the area. But this damage had not done by an elephant.

As Briget stepped onto the flattened ground, the smell hit her hard and she saw the first carcass of what might have been a deer directly in front of her. The remains of smaller animals were all around. Many were clustered in and around an opening in a rock formation.

She cautiously approached the cave. Before disappearing into the darkness, she took a breath, tightly clutching the valuable cloth in her hand. Just a few feet in, the darkness was almost complete.

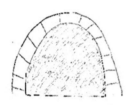

Suddenly something shot out of the black void in front of her. She ducked and it narrowly missed her head. At first, she thought it was a bat, but it landed on the ground at the mouth of the cave in a heap of feathers and blood atop a pile of small, desiccated bones. The ground beneath her began to shake and a grunting sound from deep within the cave caused her to snap her head around with great alarm. The mini earthquake was accompanied by a thunderous growl.

"Arrgghhh!"

A giant beast charged at her. She took several steps backward, delicate bones crunching under her boots. She stumbled and almost fell. While she managed to keep her balance, she dropped the cloth she was holding and her sister's diamond engagement ring slipped out, disappearing in the pile of animal bones. "Oh, no!" she cried.

"Go away!" a monstrous voice howled.

She looked up at the hulking figure and shuddered. Even in the dimness, she recognized the creature. She knew what it was only because she had heard it described. There it was, a fachan, in the flesh. A most hideous and malevolent goblin. The mere sight of the monster was said to stop a person's heart. It leered down at her with a single blood-shot eye. The creature might have been pitiable if it wasn't so revolting.

Garbhan raised the mace high, prepared to bring it down on the intruder. "How did you find me? Did Buach send you?"

"N-No," she stammered. "My name is Briget. I trade gold and other valuable objects with goblins in exchange for magic power. I have something for you." She got down on her hands and knees and sifted through the bones, which crumbled between her fingers. She searched desperately, but there was no sign of the precious gem.

"Leave now or *your* bones'll lie on top of this heap."

The tip of one finger brushed against the ring. She couldn't see it, but she was able to grasp it between her fingers and pull it out.

She stood and raised her arm. "Look." She held the prize between her thumb and forefinger to fully expose it to the giant. She swiveled her wrist slowly to try to reflect the meager light and make it sparkle. "It's a diamond. It's more valuable than the gold that it's set in. It's for you." She gritted her teeth, fighting a pang of shame for stealing her sister's wedding ring and using it to barter with an evil goblin.

The beast gazed upon the object in wonder. "For me?" The brow over its large eye furrowed. "What do I have to do?"

"I need to talk to Buach."

The mace came down swiftly, impacting the ground near her feet with tremendous force and pulverizing the animal bones to dust. "Buach!" he raged.

"Yes." She managed to maintain a steady voice. "Can you take me to his lair?"

"Impossible."

"There is special power associated with this diamond. It belongs to a human woman with goblin blood."

"What makes you think I can help you?"

"I saw a red cap," she began. "He seemed to have escaped into the human world. Someone other than Buach had to have helped the red cap. If you can put me in contact with the goblin who assisted in his escape, the diamond is yours."

"What do you want this goblin to do for you?"

"I figured the goblin who did this must be powerful and influential. So, he must be close to Buach."

"No one finds Buach." He pulled out the mighty club that was buried deep in the ground. "Buach finds *you*. This would not be pleasant. Why do you risk your life?"

"He has my sister. I believe he replaced her with a fetch. I don't have the power to see through the magic, but I saw it in my nephew's eyes. He must have special ability." She paused. Her eyes welled with tears. "You see, I have been jealous of my sister because she has goblin blood and I do not. It has made me do things that weren't right. After seeing the way my nephew looked at his mother, I've got to do something to help her, tell her I'm sorry, and reunite her with her son."

Garbhan laughed in her face. "Buach will never free any of his captives. He does not keep any promises, especially not to humans. Any promises he made to the boy will not be kept, either. He will lie and cheat and do whatever he has to do to win. If Buach has your sister, you will not see her again. That much, I can tell you."

"I don't accept that. There must be something Buach wants."

Garbhan shook his head and his whole body wobbled. "He wants everything. You have nothing to trade. He trusts no one and will kill those closest to him just as he would his enemies."

"You're scared of Buach." It was not a question.

"I'M NOT SCARED OF ANYTHING." The creature's entire body suddenly tensed, its muscles flexed, and veins popped through its thick gray skin. The fachan seemed to increase half again in size. He opened his mouth wide and bellowed fiercely. A miasma, like swamp gas, streamed from its gullet in a wave with such force that it blew Briget's hair behind her head. She recoiled as a clear, frothy film vibrated back and forth in the corner of its mouth. When he settled down, returning to normal height and width, he looked at Briget with a wide eye. "Why have you not run away? Are you not afraid of me?"

"Yes, I am very afraid" she admitted, her voice trembling even as she stood her ground. "But I still want to see my sister."

"I cannot help you. No one can."

"How can you be sure...I'm sorry, what is your name?"

Still holding the club in hand, the cyclops scratched the side of his head with it. He gazed at the human woman, his mouth slightly agape, a string of spittle hanging from his lower lip. "Garbhan," he muttered.

"Okay, Garbhan, how can you be so sure about Buach?"

"Because I was his Underlord until he decided he couldn't trust me."

"Then you can help me."

"No." Garbhan took a wary step backward. "Buach ordered Flann, the red cap that you saw, to kill me. But I struck a deal with the bloodthirsty goblin. I knew where the boy's portal was located.

I told the red cap about it and how he can use it to gain passage into the human world where, although he would have no magic or protection and could be seen by all humans, he could kill indiscriminately.

He spared my life for this knowledge and I faked my death. I mixed bamboo and hibiscus with bloodroot to dye Flann's cap red so that Buach would believe I was killed."

"See. That's just what I mean. Everybody has something they're willing to trade."

"I have nothing to trade. I used up all the magic that I had to help the red cap enter the human world."

"You're hiding, then."

"I'm surviving."

Briget stared back at him for a long moment without saying anything. Garbhan shuffled uneasily on his massive heel. "Why are you looking at me like that?"

"I was just wondering something. Why did you align yourself with him?"

"What?"

"Why did you align yourself with Buach, a goblin so warped by hatred and consumed by an insatiable craving for power?"

The fachan's brow wrinkled. "Why did you do all the things that you did, trading goods that didn't belong to you to goblins?" When she did not respond, he answered his own question. "For power."

She hung her head. "You're right. I guess we're more alike than it might seem."

Garbhan gave a cursory glance at the singular anatomical body parts he possessed, then looked back at Briget without saying a word.

"I meant that we both have a certain capacity for greed and vile behavior," she clarified. "But we also have a predisposition for kindness and compassion, and that's what always wins out in the end."

Garbhan laughed softly. "The only chance your sister has is if the Mound Men can beat Buach's baseball team tomorrow. And there is *no* chance at all of that."

"I think you're wrong." Her voice resounded with conviction. "Don't get mad at me, but I'm not going to give up. That wouldn't be who I am."

There was a muted rumbling from Garbhan's belly. "You better leave now," he said, slowly raising his club. "I'm getting hungry."

Briget let her sister's ring roll down into the palm of her hand, folding her fingers tightly around it. She took a cautious step back, and without turning completely away from the fachan, she left the creature alone in its cave.

Top of the 9th

Jake had been taken to the field along with his father in a van driven by a goblin. When they left the farmhouse, it was early morning, but the intersection between the human and goblin worlds created an alternate universe, where time and reality were not in sync. Despite it being full dark with no artificial lighting, every corner of the playing field was illuminated. The biggest, brightest full moon imaginable was positioned directly overhead. The diffuse, gray beams radiating from the celestial body bathed the earth in astral luster. Although it provided sufficient light to see by, it generated no heat. While Jake shivered, he was certain that his father, who arrived wearing a pair of sunglasses, saw a bloated summer sun in the sky.

The field was lined and immaculately prepared by a goblin grounds crew that took great pride in their work. Perfectly trimmed hedgerows ringed the outfield, creating an eight-foot-high natural fence from foul pole to foul pole. In the entire history of baseball, a more important game had never been played. It was fitting that this contest should take place in Pine Barrows, where the pastime had been conceived.

His father had his game-face on. He was focused and determined while Jake sat quietly in the dugout pounding an old baseball into his glove as he watched the players warm up before the game.

Both goblin teams were wearing full uniforms. The Order was in all black, featuring old-fashioned collar shirts. "BUACH BOMBERS" was embroidered across the front of their jerseys, the block lettering sticked within the image of a mushroom cloud rising from a smoldering baseball bat. The Bombers all got loose together, stretching and doing calisthenics as a team, counting in unison.

The Mound Men, on the other hand, were sporting steel gray uniforms that appeared to be several sizes too big for many of them. They were much smaller in stature than their opponents, their shirts and pants billowing behind them as they bounded all around the field in small groupings. Several were playing "pepper" near the backstop. Another cluster stood in a circle beside the dugout tossing a ball to each other in unusual ways, such as flipping it behind their backs, between their legs or bouncing it off the crooks of their elbows. Others were stretching and rolling around on the ground like children. Prank was doing some kind of dance while indiscriminately breaking out into cartwheels. As they were talking and laughing and having a great time, Skip looked out from the dugout at them and smiled. He reminded Jake of old pictures he had seen of Casey Stengel, the great New York Yankees manager from the 1950s. He half expected the goblin manager to lift his cap and see a bird fly out from underneath it.

"Great day for a ballgame," Skip proclaimed.

His father finished his warmups in an open bullpen along the left field line while Buach was getting ready to throw along the right field line.

"How do the boys look out there?" Skip asked Jake without turning his gaze away from the field.

Jake flinched when he realized that the goblin manager was talking to him. "They look, um, relaxed."

Skip turned to look at him. "That's important. Staying loose and not letting a big game like this get in your head. Just play. Have fun. And believe. You do that, you'll never lose."

There was a loud pop as Buach's fastball stuck the catcher's mitt on the other side of the field. The sound startled Jake, causing him to drop the ball he was holding. It rolled under the bench beneath him and out of sight. He was about to go look for it when his father and Slash walked into to the dugout together. Jake sprang up to greet them. "How do you feel, Dad?"

"To tell you the truth, sport, I feel invincible."

"We were just talking about the importance of staying loose and confident," Skip said.

"I don't know what it is, but my arm never felt this good. Even before the injury when I was at my strongest. It's weird."

"His stuff is electric today," confirmed Slash.

"That's great," Skip said. "We're almost ready to start. I'll pull our guys off the field. Jake, I'm going to need an official scorer as well as a ball boy."

"I can do it," he said excitedly. "I'm a good scorekeeper."

Indeed, he was. He was only five years old when he learned, scoring all of his father's games that he had watched.

The Order was the home team, so the Mound Men batted first. Buach came out blazing, striking out the side on nine pitches, all but one was a looking strike. He was throwing gas, and the hitters didn't have time to get the bat off their shoulders before the pitch was upon them. The third batter swung at the last pitch after the catcher caught it just to take a little shine off the 'immaculate inning.' However, it couldn't have been a more dominant start to the game for Buach and the Order.

"Let's go out there and match them zero-for-zero," Skip told his players after the top of the inning, clapping his hands enthusiastically.

His father *did* match Buach with four shutout innings, keeping the hitters off-balance by spotting his fastball and changing speeds.

His most effective pitch was his slider, which bore in on the left-handed batters. He broke numerous bats, producing a lot of easy outs. Neither pitcher allowed a hit until the fifth inning.

Buach became increasing upset because he was pitching so well but still not winning. He blamed his teammates for their inability to score. Each inning he became more incensed. He threatened his players with violence, banishment and even death if they did not start hitting the ball. After a knocker took a nasty curveball for a called strike three to end the fourth inning, Buach broke a bat over the head of the goblin. Then he threw the pieces of wood at the two other batters who grounded out that inning.

That was a turning point of sorts as Buach's anger affected not only his pitching, but the fielding of the position players behind him. His frustration caused him to lose command of his pitches. He walked the first two batters to start the fifth, hit the next one with a pitch, and with the bases loaded two consecutive infield errors allowed the first runs of the game to score. The players were so nervous and afraid of making a mistake that they were not able to play to the best of their ability. The failure caused more distress for Buach and additional anxiety for his players. They had difficulty making the easiest of plays. By the time the top of the inning was over, the Mound Men scored seven unearned runs.

Buach stalked off the mound after finally recording the third out of the inning with a punch out. The other players scattered as he entered the dugout, his tail whipping against the side wall. The thick, muscular appendage struck the concrete with great force, sending chunks of concrete and dust everywhere. He threw his glove at the goblin closest to him.

"I'm pitching a no-hitter and I'm losing 7-0," he yelled, loud enough for everyone in the park to hear. "How can that be? I'll tell you how, it's because you guys can't hit or field a ground ball, that's how."

In the other dugout, Skip turned to Jake and said, "What did I tell you. You can't win being a player who only cares about yourself. Was I right?"

"You sure were," Jake answered as he finished scoring the inning by writing "7" in the top of the 5th. He felt good writing it because it was a lucky number, and as the game went into the 7th inning with the same score, he started to believe that the Mound Men were actually going to pull off the upset. He couldn't help thinking about his mother in the cell, and how she would soon be free. If he got to see her when she awoke, he wondered what he would say to her. He thought he would probably just hug her and hold her tightly. That was all he wanted.

As his mind wandered, he noticed that hundreds of goblins had gathered around the field to watch the game. Still more were streaming in from all parts of the surrounding forest. Their collective voices resonated into an excited, raucous hum. They were clearly enjoying themselves. He also observed that the moon had been replaced by a rising sun in a magnificent azure blue sky.

His father sat down beside him and looked out at what was going on in the field, watching the action with eyes that were narrowed in sharp focus. This wasn't the first time he had been in the dugout with his father, who was always serious and intense when he was pitching, but Jake didn't think he had ever seen his father this locked-in before. It was almost as if his father knew what was on the line, and he was putting his heart and soul into every pitch. In reality, that was what he did all the time. That's what made him such a great pitcher, and able to compete with the best baseball players in the world, including the best players in the goblin world, as well.

As he sat there, Jake saw his father hitching his right shoulder and rotating it slowly as if trying to keep it loose.

"Dad, are you okay?"

"Fine, sport," his father responded without looking at him or changing his expression, even as he continued to roll his shoulder.

Buach struck out the leadoff hitter to start the 7th inning. There was some unenthusiastic cheering from the crowd, but more predominant were the cautious jeers directed at Buach, who was visibly irritated by the increasing number of onlookers who had turned against him. The fans became more vocal and emboldened, booing when a strike was called against a Mound Men hitter and clapping when it was a ball.

When Buach didn't get the call on a 3-2 pitch that just missed the outside corner, he jumped off the ground. "THAT

HIT THE CORNER!" he screamed, charging the umpire. "ARE YOU BLIND?"

The umpire, a boggart named Giggleswick, raised his long arms over his head and signaled for a time out. "No, no." The goblin official shook his head in denial. "It was off the plate."

Giggleswick had been picked personally by Buach to ump the game. He was human-like in form, short, round, and hairy, but he had the keenest eyes of any goblin in the Pine Barrows.

Buach pressed his face right up against Giggleswick's mask and a heated argument ensued. It went on for several minutes, and during that time the sky grew brighter still, the sun's rays bathing the field in bright light and radiating the spectators in its warm embrace.

Buach eventually calmed down enough to get back on the mound, and play resumed. With one out and one on in the top of the 7th, a seven-run lead seemed secure, but Skip wanted to push this run across the plate. He could see that his father was tiring. He had been getting hit harder each inning, managing to scatter the hits he gave up and getting timely outs without surrendering a run.

Slash was up next, and Skip relayed a complicated series of signals to his third base coach, Jimmy Squarefoot, who translated them very differently for the hitter. Slash watched the bipedal pig-headed creature stomp his large feet in the dirt and squeal shrilly. His elongated snout thrashed against the upturned tusks jutting from either side of his lower jaw.

Slash acknowledged the sign with a simple nod of his head and stepped into the box.

"Watch for a bunt," Buach cautioned his infielders.

Slash squared around before the pitch was delivered. Anticipating this, Buach reared back and threw the ball as hard as he could. The hitter was just looking to make contact, but the sizzling fastball struck the bat with such force that it completely shattered upon impact. The solid ash bat looked like it had been through a buzz saw, reduced to splinters on the ground around home plate.

The ball, however, landed in fair territory, not far up the third base line. Buach pointed to the ball and called to his catcher, who did not see it at first. Finally, Buach went to get the ball himself, but his catcher got there at the same time and they banged into each other. The ball got kicked away, rolling off into foul territory.

The lead runner, seeing the confusion, rounded second base and headed for third. The catcher, who finally picked up the ball, heaved it ahead of the runner. The throw was high, and it sailed into left field.

Jimmy Squarefoot wind-milled his right arm around, waving the runner home.

The outfielder was backing up the base and was in perfect position to field the ball. He made a perfect throw to plate and the catcher tagged the runner on a close play. The catcher spun around to get the call from the umpire.

"He's OUT!" The ump said as he raised the thumb of his right hand and drew his arm back emphatically.

As the catcher raised the mitt cradling the ball in triumph and started to walk off the field, Buach was gesturing maniacally to get his attention and screaming, "That's only two outs! That's only two outs!"

The dumbfounded catcher turned back toward the field of play, but it was too late. Slash, who never stopped running, slid safely across the plate before the catcher could react.

The crowd erupted. The applause was loud enough to drown out Buach's rantings as he stomped around the mound and kicked dirt.

No one was more excited than the skipper of the Mound Men. He came out of the dugout and raised his four-fingered right hand. "Give me four."

Slash, who also only had four fingers on his hands, reached up to give his manager a high-four. As soon as he stepped into the dugout, he was instantly mobbed by his teammates.

"You can't teach speed," Skip said, clapping his oversized hands. "That's a big run, fellas."

Enraged, Buach fired the next three pitches for strikes, all exceeding 110 miles per hour, to end the inning. They were his best fastballs of the game, but his team was now down 8-0 entering the seventh inning stretch.

Jake's father got through the inning, allowing only a ground rule double on a ball that was hit so hard by Buach that it smashed straight through the hedgerow wall in center field. He was left stranded there, however, and after the Mound Men went down 1-2-3 in the top of the eighth, his father got off to a rough start in the bottom half of the inning, surrendering a leadoff single, followed by a walk. He fell behind 2-0 on the next batter, but he was able to bear down and work his way out of trouble. He induced a hard-hit ground ball double play, followed by a line out to left field to end the threat without giving up a run. He had pitched eight scoreless innings.

When he came off the mound at the end of the inning, his jaw was clenched tight and he was holding his right arm across his stomach instead of letting it hang down by his side. Something was clearly wrong. Jake didn't want to ask him about it, but he thought someone should. Skip, along with the trainer, was occupied tending to the left fielder, whose hand was injured when he caught the screaming line drive. The goblin was hurt bad and had to be removed from the game.

Buach mowed down the Mound Men again in the 9th, although he struck two batters with first-pitch fastballs. The beanballs appeared intentional, and Skip and the Mound Men protested while the crowd booed and sneered robustly.

"They were brush-back pitches that got away from me," Buach lied. He seemed to take extra delight in hitting them hard enough that they needed to be helped off the field.

His father bravely took the mound to start the final frame, gutting out his warmup pitches and wincing in pain after each one. None were hard enough to break a pane of glass. Jake couldn't bear to watch as the leadoff hitter dug his back foot into the batter's box. His father went into his windup and was about to release the first pitch of the inning when he stopped his motion abruptly and yelled out in pain. The ball fell from his hand and rolled a few feet away as he dropped to his knees holding his right shoulder with his left hand.

"Dad!" Jake tossed the scorebook aside and ran out to his father, followed by Skip and the entire team. They all gathered around the mound. No one said a word. The crowd was silent, as well. Even Jake didn't know what to say.

"I came up a little short," his father said with a lagging smile. He looked at Jake. "I gave it my all, sport."

"You did great, Dad."

"You don't know just how great of a performance that was," Skip interjected. "To shut out a team like that for eight innings. I've never seen it done before. But the job's not done." The goblin manager turned his gaze upon Jake. "We need someone to close this thing out.

Jake's eyes went wide. "Me? You want me to pitch against these guys."

"I don't have anyone else," Skip informed him. "Buach hit eight of my players, and seven of them aren't able to play. You're all we got. We need you."

"You can do it, sport." His father leaned down and picked up the ball with his left hand and gave it to his son.

Jake looked at the ball and then back at his father. "I'll try."

His father smiled and nodded. "You can do it. I believe in you. This team believes in you."

"Thanks, Dad." He swallowed hard and thought about his mother. He would do it. For her.

Skip grinned, seeing something no one else did. It was confidence and a look of determination that was strong enough to withstand any challenge no matter how daunting.

Bottom of the 9th

The crowd had swelled considerably. There were thousands of goblins surrounding the field and many more clustered in the surrounding trees. They came in droves. Goblins that had been in hiding. Goblins from other territories. They heard about the baseball game and came out to watch the grand contest. They were loud and boisterous, munching on wild nuts and berries. Some were roasting rabbits on open flames. They were drinking grog made from the nectar of flowers.

The first batter Jake faced in a live game was not another 11-year-old kid, which alone was a prospect that once terrified him, but a supernatural beast that played baseball at an extremely high level. The bugbear stood six feet tall, with a brown shaggy coat, broad head, extended jaw, and other features like a bear.

Hitting from the left side of the plate, the bulky goblin was sixty feet six inches away from Jake, but he seemed much closer. Jake's opponent's yellow eyes studied him, slather dripping from the corner of its mouth. He tried to keep his eyes on the target, Slash's mitt, rather than what was occupying the entire batter's box. The noise of the crowd increased in anticipation of the pitch. It rose to a deafening level as Slash put down one finger, which Jake acknowledged with a nod. He took a deep breath and went into his windup, unleashing a four-seam fastball. He knew he had to keep it away, and he hit his spot, but the bugbear covered the plate and hit a towering fly ball that sailed high over the right field foul pole. The umpire watched it the whole way, but didn't make the call right away, finally signaling that it was a fair ball. The home run put the Buach Bombers on the board, now trailing 8-1.

The crowd quieted a bit, but they didn't seem worried. Skip and the Mound Men players voiced their encouragement and support to Jake.

"That wasn't you," Slash told him. "You made a perfect pitch. He put a good swing on it. Don't worry about it. Get the next one."

Jake got a fresh ball from the umpire and saw Buach make his way to the plate. He was grinning, and he made sure his opposing pitcher was looking at him. Before settling into his stance, he looked out into centerfield, rested the bat on his shoulder, and raised his opposite hand. He pointed a finger out toward deep center field, calling his shot.

"Come on, kid," Slash said. "You got this." This time, a breaking pitch was called. Jake took another deep breath and spun a tight curve ball. Buach seemed to know what was coming. He waited and timed the pitch perfectly, hitting a moonshot out of the park in the exact spot he had pointed. He watched the ball leave the yard, then flipped his bat, sending is spiraling straight up into the sky. It kept going until it disappeared from sight. The Overlord jogged extra slowly around the bases, the boos growing louder during his relaxed homerun trot. As he rounded second base, the bat reappeared, tumbling down toward the ground, twirling end of end. Buach stepped on the plate and looked up, catching the bat in front of him before turning to Jake on the mound.

"You tipped your pitch, otherkin," he scoffed, then turned and strutted toward the dugout.

It was 8-2, but the tide was turning. Jake felt all alone out there. He felt completely isolated after he surrendered homeruns to the next four batters. Each one was hit further than the one before. After giving up six consecutive dingers, the Mound Men's eight-run lead had been cut to two. Jake called time out and stepped off the mound. He didn't want to be the one to lose the game and everything else to Buach.

Skip came out to talk to him.

"I can't do this," Jake said and handed the ball to the manager. "I don't have anything to get these guys out. They're too good."

"You're every bit as good as they are," Skip assured him.

"Yeah," Slash agreed. "They just got lucky."

Jake looked at him sideways. "They got lucky *six times?*"

Skip clasped his four-fingered hands on Jake's shoulder and forced him to look directly at him. "I know I don't have to tell you what's riding on this," he began, "but if you don't finish this game, we forfeit everything to Buach. You can't give up. This entire crowd, your father, and your teammates all want to see you try to get these last three outs."

Jake glanced at his father, who was wearing a makeshift sling on his arm and watching from the dugout, then turned to Skip and took the ball back from him. "Three outs," he repeated.

"You got the bottom of the order coming up," Skip informed him.

"Let's do it," Slash said and patted his glove on Jake's shoulder before jogging back behind the plate.

When play resumed, Jake worked a 2-2 count on the shortstop, Finbar. He thought he had him, but the very next pitch was driven out of the park, just out of reach of the right fielder beyond the hedgerow. The lively trow seemed to have more fun than anyone, giggling uncontrollably as he made his way around the bases.

Jake had been taken deep seven times in a row and it was now just a one-run game.

It's not over, he told himself. *Just need three outs.*

After Finbar crossed the plate, the umpire raised his arms and called time out. "I'm out of baseballs," he announced. "Does anyone have a baseball?"

Skip and Buach came out of their respective dugouts to inform the ump that they did not.

"I'll have to suspend the game," the umpire said.

"No," Jake objected. His mother did not have any more time. "I have a ball. It's under the bench in the dugout."

Skip instructed his players to have a look around the dugout. Prank found it and looked at it closely. "This old thing?" he commented, then tossed it to Skip.

"It will have to do," the manager of the Mound Men said, rubbing the ball up. Suddenly he did a doubletake when he got a good look at it. His eyes widened as he turned it over in his hand several times.

Jake walked over to foul line near home plate where Skip was standing, examining the ball with great interest. "What's wrong?"

"Where did you get this?" the goblin manager asked him in a low, conspiratorial tone.

Jake's brow furrowed in confusion as he looked at the ball Skip was holding, and then his jaw nearly came unhinged when he realized what it was. "Is that...?"

Skip's piercing gaze and silent headshake warned him not to say anymore.

It was magnificent. There was a faint iridescent glow along the seams. Jake couldn't believe that the baseball was what everyone had been searching Pine Barrows for. He had found it in the basement, inside one of the boxes of junk. It just seemed like an old baseball, so he picked it up and put in his pocket without giving it a second thought. It was only by chance that he had taken it with him to the game.

"Let me see that," the umpire said as he approached them.

"Don't say anything," Skip whispered out of the side of his mouth. "Only you can see the magic it possesses." He lobbed the ball to the umpire, who inspected it briefly before tossing it to Jake.

"PLAY BALL!"

It was hard for Jake not to stare at the ball as he positioned his fingers along the faintly glowing stitches, which radiated a mild surge of energy that ran from his hand, up his arm, to his shoulder. Standing on the pitcher's mound now, he was more confident, though not sure what was going to happen. He took a deep breath as the next batter stepped in. The first pitch he threw was popped straight up. It was a mile high, and the third baseman, Bud Reedtwist, called for it. He positioned himself in front of the bag and caught the ball when it eventually came down.

The fans, finally with something to cheer about, let their voices be heard. Jake was startled by the roar of crowd. A chant rose slowly – *TWO MORE OUTS* – and then grew louder by degrees.

TWO MORE OUTS!

TWO MORE OUTS!

This invigorated Jake. He felt their energy, and in possession of the Sacred Amulet and all its magic, he was sure he could get the number nine hitter out. A knocker walked to the plate. He had a bandage wrapped around his head, which Buach had broken a bat over earlier in the game.

Jake threw a fastball that rode in high and tight, knocking the knocker on his butt. The crowd reacted with raucous applause. The cheering intensified further when the next pitch, a sweeping curve, was swung at weakly and missed.

"That's how you work those corners," Skip said, clapping.

With a 1-1 count, the batter guessed fastball but got another curve ball. Out in front of the pitch, the goblin rolled over it, hitting a slow roller to short that was gobbled up by Yarrow Heartwasp, who threw to first in plenty of time for the second out of the inning.

ONE MORE OUT!

Jake could barely hear himself think.

ONE MORE OUT!

Freeing his mother seemed to be within reach now, even though the top of the order was coming up, beginning with the bugbear, who started the inning off with a long ball.

Jake blocked out everything as he faced down a monster that was growling at him under its breath. Jake's eyes and his entire focus were on one thing: Slash's mitt. Taking in a lungful of air, he held it for a moment and then released it. The two-seamer he delivered broke just late enough to fool the batter. It caught too much of the plate, however, and although the bugbear wasn't able to square the ball up, getting a little underneath it, he hit a humpback liner into the gap in left-center field. It stayed in the park, but the tying run was at second base with a standing double.

Jake got the ball back and straddled the pitching rubber as Buach strode to the plate, grinning and twirling his massive bat on his shoulder. The Overlord dug into batter's box and tapped his bat on the plate. Looking up at Jake, he told him with a cocky sneer, "I'll be touching this same spot with my foot after I hit the game-winning home run."

Slash pounded his mitt to keep Jake's focus on the target. The catcher gave a sign and a location. Jake nodded and drew in a deep breath. This was it.

Wanting to establish control of the plate, Jake threw a high fastball that clipped the inside corner for a strike.

Buach watched it go by without making any attempt to lift the bat off his shoulder.

Jake followed that pitch up with a big sweeping curveball for strike two. Again, the Overlord stood frozen in place, grinning.

Jake was just one strike away from winning the game for the Mound Men. When he received the ball back from the catcher, Buach extended his arm once again, pointing to a spot in the distant woods beyond left field. The crowd reacted harshly, jeering and razzing him.

Jake maintained his focus, looking in for his sign as Buach got into his batting stance. Slash called for a changeup, but Jake shook it off immediately. Slash put it down again and Jake shook it off again. He did not have confidence that he could throw the pitch as effectively as his breaking ball. The catcher looked into the dugout at Skip, then gave the sign more emphatically. Jake hesitated, but finally nodded. Breathing deeply, he got into the set position from the stretch.

The crowd was on their feet. Everyone was hollering and screaming.

While the count was not in Buach's favor, the Overlord did not show any concern. He was spoiling to end the game with a walk off home run. He had already imagined it happening in his mind. But Jake had other plans. He reached back for a little something more and uncorked what looked to be a fastball when it left his hand. The ball was headed straight down the middle. Buach's eyes flared wide in anticipation. He started his swing, but by then the ball had already begun to cut down and in on him, and he could not make an adjustment in time.

"Oh, no," Buach muttered softly as he swung and missed.

"Striiiiiiiii-ke thr-eeeeee," the umpire called, pumping his fist emphatically as the goblin crowd erupted all at once and began to stream onto the field.

Buach stood in the batter's box bewildered, and as the reality of what just happened settled in, he became furious. "I order every one of you back," he howled venomously.

Something unexpected happened. No one listened. The goblins rejoiced, jumped up and down in celebration. Several of them hoisted Jake up onto their shoulders and paraded him around in victory. His father was among them, supporting his son with his good shoulder.

"You did it, sport. I knew you could."

"Thanks Dad. You always believed in me. You got me to believe in myself."

He smiled when he spotted Lorcan chewing a mouthful of gum and blowing bubbles. "Lorcan. You're back."

"I wouldn't have missed this for anything," Lorcan said. "What a game! What a pitch!"

The Overlord gasped when he looked up at the sun-drenched sky. His dark powers had been drained during the course of the game. He was so focused on winning that he wasn't aware it was happening. He had stolen the power from the goblins of Pine Barrows and held onto it by banishing baseball, but they had won it back. The heart of the game was something that could never be eradicated. The human boy had seen to that.

There was something even more unusual that happened to Buach then. The fire in his eyes dimmed to dull embers before being snuffed out completely, revealing lucid bright green irises. He was no longer angry. He was disappointed that the game had not gone the way he wanted, but he was actually anxious to play again and hopeful for the next game when he would have a chance to redeem himself. Which was what the game of baseball was all about, hope and redemption. The thrill of competition and his love of the game had been restored.

Buach knew what had happened but he didn't know how it could have been achieved with the goblin community lacking a queen. The power he had lost had to go somewhere. It did not make sense to him until he looked up as a reverential silence spread over the crowd. The goblins of Pine Barrows parted to allow a woman on horseback to ride onto the field. She was wearing a beautiful green gown and sitting sidesaddle astride a black horse. Trailing behind her were all the goblins that Buach had imprisoned. They were free, their cell doors dissolved by the enduring power and magic of baseball.

"Mom!" Jake called out. He scrambled down off the shoulders of the goblins and raced to the mound, where Ruadhan and his mother stopped. "It's you. It's really you."

She smiled as the horse lowered its back legs to allow her to dismount. Jake leapt into her open arms. His father joined them, putting his arms around both of them. They held that embrace for a long time before Jake slowly pulled back, his brows knitted above curious eyes that surveyed her long flowing gown. The cape she wore, buttoned under her neck was a much darker green than the dress. "Mom, what is all this?"

"I'm going to take your place in the goblin world," she informed him. "I'm going to act as their queen."

"No," he protested. "We won. You're free."

"It's okay. It'll only be here for a little while, until they find a permanent queen. And you will be able to visit. Both you and your father can visit me anytime you want."

Her smile made everything okay, the way it always had. He smiled back. Suddenly Lorcan wandered by and Jake called out to him.

"Mom, I want you to meet my friend, Lorcan."

The hogboon bowed at the waist. "Please to meet you, Your Royal Highness."

Jake and his mother and father looked at one other, then started to laugh while all around them goblins continued to celebrate the victory. Remarkably, Buach was among them, showing a group of goblins how he throws his cut fastball.

"The others don't have a heavy tail they can use for counterbalance during the delivery like he does," his father commented as he observed Buach.

Jake's jaw dropped a little. "You can see them?"

"I can now. Since the magic wore off."

"This is for you," Skip said. Jake turned and saw the manager of the Mound Men standing beside him holding the game ball in his hand. "Go ahead and take it. You deserve it."

"I can't take the Sacred Amulet."

"Who said it was the Sacred Amulet?"

"What?"

"The Sacred Amulet cannot be possessed by anyone," Skip revealed.

Jake's eyes went wide. "You mean I did it myself?'

"It's just a regular old baseball," Skip told him.

Jake took the ball and examined it but found no trace of the glowing laces. He looked up at Skip. "You used magic to make me see it."

"You said you always believed that magic existed," Skip said. "That's all you have to do. Believe. That's the real magic."

Jake stared back at Skip, speechless.

The goblin manager grasped Jake by the shoulder. "You can play for me anytime. But I have a feeling you'll be doing a lot of that in the human world. Keep working, kid." He gave Jake a pat on the back before walking away.

"I'm proud of you, son," his father said.

His mother leaned forward and gave him a kiss on the forehead. "Me, too."

Jake smiled. She didn't smell like wet leaves. She just smelled like mom.

Postgame

Jake learned that his parents didn't know that the other had goblin blood, so neither of them considered the effect that his supernatural ancestry might have on him. They never told each other about their experiences and abilities to observe goblin activities because they didn't want to scare the other away or be thought of as crazy.

His mother was a beautiful queen, and he did get to see her whenever he wanted. All the goblins who had fled felt safe and returned to Pine Barrows. There were so many of them and they all liked playing baseball. Jake played with them all summer and had a lot of fun.

Then the day came when his mother announced that she was not going to be queen anymore. She gave the crown and all its trappings to Aunt Briget, but only if her sister promised that she would be fair and just. It worked out perfectly for everyone. Being a queen was just what Aunt Briget always wanted, and Jake and his mom and dad got to be a family again. The goblins of Pine Barrows really liked Briget for her persuasive ways and the knack she had for dealing with difficult individuals. She was able to settle the small disputes that arose between goblin factions before they turned into big problems.

Jake and his family moved back to New York, renting a house in Astoria. His father retired from baseball and worked with his brothers in the family construction business. Jake joined a fall youth baseball league and played very well. He led his team in every pitching category and even threw a no-hitter. Otherwise, life went pretty much back to normal. His perception of the supernatural world was greatly muted by all the human interference and activities of big city life. However, the limitations of the magic that separated the goblin world from the human world was exposed one November day when a counselor at a campground in upstate New York reported sighting of a strange creature stalking through the woods. His account made the local news and was later picked up by national media outlets. The counselor managed to snap a picture of the creature that at first was thought to be Bigfoot. The grainy photo, however, revealed something else entirely. This hairy monster was wearing iron boots and carrying a long pike. A bright red cap fit snugly on its head, and anybody who saw the picture thought that the creature was not of this world. And they were right.

Jake recognized the creature instantly, and he realized that Flann must have escaped from the goblin world through the portal he had constructed. He couldn't let the murderous goblin terrorize people or do something much worse. It would be his fault. He had to do something.

And there was only one thing he could do.

He had to go back to Pine Barrows.

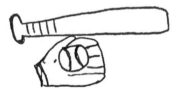

THE END

CPSIA information can be obtained
at www.ICGtesting.com
Printed in the USA
LVHW080359180621
690564LV00032B/1741/J

9 781736 701607